S0-CWS-332

"I WANT TO MAKE LOVE TO YOU."

She averted her face slightly, and her eyes clouded. Rod was the most physically beautiful man she had ever seen. She knew that countless other women agreed. . . . Perhaps Rod had so many women standing in line that seducing them thoughtlessly had become nothing more than a pleasant hobby to him.

His hand began to gently trace the outline of her bikini bra, and all the caution and uncertainty was swept away in a blinding surge of overpowering longing. She turned back to him and let her eyes drink in every part of the face above her: the dampened black ringlets, the strong dark brows, the hypnotic eyes, the full, slightly parted lips.

She was unable to resist him.

CANDLELIGHT ECSTASY ROMANCES™

THAT ISLAND, THAT SUMMER

Belle Thorne

A CANDLELIGHT ECSTASY ROMANCE™

Published by
Dell Publishing Co., Inc.
1 Dag Hammarskjold Plaza
New York, New York 10017

Dell® TM 681510, Dell Publishing Co., Inc.

Candlelight Ecstasy Romance™ is a trademark of
Dell Publishing Co., Inc., New York, New York.

ISBN: 0-440-18725-7

Printed in the United States of America

First printing—January 1982

Dear Reader:

In response to your enthusiasm for Candlelight Ecstasy Romances™, we are now increasing the number of titles per month from three to four.

We are pleased to offer you sensuous novels set in America depicting modern American women and men as they confront the provocative problems of a modern relationship.

Throughout the history of the Candlelight line, Dell has tried to maintain a high standard of excellence, to give you the finest in reading pleasure. It is now and will remain our most ardent ambition.

Editor
Candlelight Romances

THAT ISLAND, THAT SUMMER

Chapter 1

Years later Melissa Starbuck could still evoke an echo of the emotions that warred within her heart the first time she saw Rod Wilshire.

She was biking down South Beach Street in Nantucket Town. It was not yet ten o'clock on a fine day in early June, and the water lapping into Steamboat Wharf in the wake of the ferry smelled deliciously briny. The last remaining wisps of early-morning fog were proving no match for the strengthening sun, and even the slight jarring of her bicycle wheels on the cobblestones became pleasantly monotonous.

Exuberantly accelerating her speed, she nursed a smug feeling of triumph, for her father's instructions of the previous evening had been specific:

"If we're going to advertise Highcliffe Inn's gourmet food, let's try to live up to our claims. I'm not going to tear up a piece of iceberg lettuce and call it a salad. So find some good avocados, never mind how expensive they are."

Lissa smiled as she glanced at the half-dozen rich green fruits in her bike basket. She had had to try three markets to find just-ripe ones, but these were perfect.

She was so pleased with her shopping coup that she did not at first notice the tall man with the duffel bag who had just disembarked from the Woods Hole Ferry. By the time she realized that he had not seen her and was crossing the street directly in her path, it was too late. She hit the brakes with all her force, but both she and her precious cargo were thrown to the street as the bike collided head-on with the solidly packed duffel bag.

Furious, she got to her knees, realizing with relief that only her dignity was injured. She brushed off her yellow shorts and started collecting the avocados, examining each one carefully to assess the damage. She heard a rude snort of stifled laughter above her and jerked her head up. Standing over her, an avocado in each outstretched hand, his duffel bag carelessly discarded at the curb, was the most handsome man she had ever laid eyes on. He was thirtyish; coal-black hair tumbled over his forehead in a mass of disheveled curls. From the deep bronze of his face wicked blue eyes and dazzling teeth stood out in stunning relief.

But his physical attributes held no charm for her at the moment—not, at least, on any conscious level. The emotion that took over was rage. She stood up and glared at him. He was a full head taller than she, a humiliating fact she did her best to ignore.

"Does it amuse you to cross the street without looking?" she asked, her voice heavy with sarcasm. She impatiently flung back a lock of brick-red hair that had escaped her visored cap. "Give me those avocados, please, and let me see if they're ruined completely." She continued grumbling as she felt the fruit gingerly. "I've spent half the morning trying to find these damn things for our guests."

"Whoa!" The man laughed. "Public swearing? And from such a tiny mite?"

Melissa's green eyes flashed with anger. She did not like to be reminded of her five-three petiteness, especially not by someone who must have been at least six feet tall. From adolescence Melissa's dearest fantasy was miraculously to blossom upward into a willowy five seven or eight.

Oblivious to her internal fuming, the man continued: "If they could hear your language, the founding fathers of this island would surely spin in their graves. They were very pious Quakers, you know."

10

"You deserve to hear much worse," she muttered. "And I don't need a lecture in Nantucket history from some off-islander who's just set foot here."

"That could be an unwarranted assumption," he retorted. "How do you know I wasn't born and bred here?"

"You don't look the type," she snapped, eyeing his three-button business suit.

"As it happens, this is my first trip. But that's neither here nor there." His air of relaxed carelessness heightened her fury, but he continued undaunted: "You know, you must surely have been exceeding the speed limit on that thing. You came at me like a demon."

Now he was arrogantly trying to put her on the defensive. But she decided to say nothing, refusing to give his remarks the dignity of an answer.

"Well?" he asked, indicating the avocados she had wrested from his hands, "did they survive the assault? If not, I'll replace them if you'll tell me where you got them." The grin had disappeared, but there was still a suspicious twitching at the corners of his mouth.

"Oh, forget it," she said, declining his offer ungraciously. "They're okay, I think."

She gave herself another brief dust-off and mounted the bicycle, giving her nemesis a sidewise parting glance of disdain. As she made a left turn into Whalers' Lane she looked back to check for oncoming traffic. The man had picked up his duffel bag and was staring after her. When he saw her turn back, he grinned and waved an outrageously exaggerated good-bye.

By the time Lissa turned onto Cliff Road, the smell of sharp salt air, mingled with the subtle perfume of lilacs and early roses, had soothed her spirits and restored her earlier buoyancy. Melissa's fiery temper usually vanished as quickly as it appeared. On the gray clapboard porch of Highcliffe Inn her mother was instructing two workmen who were installing coachmen's lamps on either side of the

11

main entrance. A trim blue-jeaned figure, Ellen Starbuck, waved a casual greeting as she saw Lissa pedal up the hill.

"Did you get the avocados, darling?" Ellen asked her daughter. "Oh, good, I see you did. Do you think we should use pink or white bulbs in these lamps?"

"I like pink," Lissa answered immediately.

"Yes, I think so, too. Gives a warmer glow, doesn't it?" She nodded to one of the workmen. "We'll use the pink, Jason. And I think that height is about right—just a bit above eye level." Then to Lissa: "I haven't waked your father yet, but he should be down soon."

"Did he have trouble sleeping again last night?" Lissa asked alertly as they left the porch and crossed the big central lounge area.

"He said not, but I heard him get up twice, so I imagine he's being a little bit less than truthful." Ellen Starbuck's soft Virginia drawl took on a concerned tone. "When I got up to come downstairs, he roused and said he'd be right behind me, but he'd fallen asleep again before I left the room. So I guess he spent a kind of restless night."

Lissa frowned with anxiety. The state of Paul Starbuck's health was more precarious than even Ellen knew. Her mother went behind the check-in desk to take care of some paperwork, and Lissa continued into the long, narrow kitchen where Sally and Marie, the two capable townswomen, were preparing lunch for the Highcliffe guests.

"Hi, Sally. What can I do to help with lunch?"

The white-aproned woman indicated the avocados Melissa was placing carefully on the bleached-wood table. "Looks like you got your hands full already."

"No, these are for dinner tonight, with the shrimp."

Sally Emerson went to a stainless-steel refrigerator and returned with a large bowl of cooked chicken. "Then if you will, honey, take this chicken off the bones and cut it up bite-size. Your dad'll want to take it from there, I expect."

12

"I'm sure." Lissa smiled and settled herself to work, sitting on a stool well out of the way of the two bustling women. Her mind returned to her father. He must have passed a very uncomfortable night to be sleeping so late this morning; she hoped he hadn't overworked. Now she thought back to that blustery February day four months ago when she had gone determinedly to Dr. Spangler's office in New York.

"I have to know, Dr. Spangler. How sick is my father? He and Mother are determined to move to Nantucket and take over the management of that old hotel." Dr. Spangler nodded as she spoke. "It'll need quite a bit of work, and if he isn't capable of doing it, I want to be there to help out."

Thoughtful, Dr. Spangler doodled on a note pad. He had been the Starbucks' family doctor for years and knew the streak of stubbornness common to both father and daughter.

"Lissa, you have your own life. You can't just walk out on your job—your own career." For almost a year Melissa had had a running role on one of television's most popular daytime programs, *To Dare to Live.*

She interrupted him: "But that's exactly why I'm asking you now. If I give the writers and producers enough notice and tell them the circumstances, they can write me out of the show for a few months and write me back in when summer's over. They're very good about cooperating, provided they have time to do it. So you've got to be frank with me."

Dr. Spangler gave a long sigh and nodded acquiescence. He reached behind him into a file drawer and extracted a buff folder tabbed with her father's name. He interrupted his review of it with a sudden question: "Exactly what did your father tell you after his—after we found out about his heart problem?"

"Oh, he made light of it all. You know Dad. He just said

13

you advised him to walk instead of run, and get out of the advertising business for a while."

"And why did you suspect there was more?"

"Because I've watched him a couple of times when he didn't know I was looking."

Dr. Spangler nodded briefly. "I see. The heart muscles are somewhat weakened." He added hastily, "Your father could live to be a hundred and ten, Melissa. But he should be careful not to overexert himself."

Lissa smoothed a wrinkle in her gray tweed skirt. "Do you think taking over that hotel is a good idea for him, then, Dr. Spangler?"

The doctor rested his chin on his folded hands. "Well, there's no question that Nantucket is far more easygoing than New York City. And he'll be doing what he enjoys. But he will have to be persuaded to curtail any hard physical labor. And considering how active—and mule-headed, I might add—he's always been, that might not be an easy matter."

"I know. And Mother is far too gentle with him. She can be a hellion at times with anyone else, but not with Dad." Lissa's eyes softened as she thought of her mother's fierce protectiveness toward Paul Starbuck. "Well, thank you, Doctor." She rose and put on her coat. "You've helped me make my decision."

"Which is—?"

"I'm going to ask the program writer to let my character conveniently disappear for a few months, and I'm going to spend the summer in Nantucket."

Now Lissa's retrospective excursion was cut short as Paul Starbuck entered the kitchen. He spoke genially to Sally and Marie, then came to Melissa's corner.

"Any coffee left for an old slugabed who doesn't leave his couch till the disgraceful hour of ten thirty?" He tied on his chef's apron as he spoke.

Lissa laughed. "I think there's some in the family pot." The guests were served from an enormous stainless-steel urn, but between meals an ancient blue-speckled enamel percolator was kept warming on the back of the range. "I'll get you some."

Her father raised a protesting hand. "No, no. You keep working on that chicken. I'm always glad to see someone else do the slave labor and leave the fun for me."

Fine cooking had always been one of Paul Starbuck's passions and taking over Highcliffe Inn would give him a chance to indulge himself freely. Another attraction in leasing the old hotel had been Nantucket itself, the island of his birth. And a third reason was his favorite outdoor sport, sailing.

Lissa watched him surreptitiously as he poured coffee into a big earthenware mug. Was she imagining that he looked a trifle pale? "Want some breakfast, Dad?"

"No—no, I have to get busy with lunch. I wish your mother had waked me—there are things I should have been doing this morning."

"Like what?"

"Like seeing that those steps down to the beach get repaired. I know nobody's swimming this early in the season, but a little later somebody could get hurt."

"The lumber's been ordered and the steps have been roped off until they're fixed."

Paul raised his eyebrows in surprise. "Who saw to that? I hadn't even mentioned it—"

"Oh, I took a walk yesterday and noticed they looked a little dilapidated around the edges. Jason helped me measure them this morning and told me where to order the lumber."

Her father ran a hand through his thick sandy hair and smiled indulgently at his daughter. "You're putting your old father out of a job, you're so efficient. I can't find anything to do anymore except fiddle around here in the kitchen."

"That's just as it should be," she said teasingly. "You

15

stay in the kitchen and let the ladies take care of the carpentry. Makes a nice change in the order of things."

"Well, I don't know. Can't let the ladies get too far out of hand. Heaven only knows what that would lead to."

Lissa looked at him with an adoring smile. Paul Starbuck often pretended to be the worst sort of male chauvinist, but his advertising agency had been known as one of the best in the business for treating women with impeccable fairness. His blustering macho posture was so diametrically opposed to his real nature that it had become something of a family joke.

The chicken boned and cubed, Melissa handed the bowl to her father. "What else do you need?" she asked, glancing at the row of ingredients he was assembling.

"Let's see . . . orange peel, sherry, butter—you might snip a few sprigs of parsley and chives for me. You'll probably have to get some from the herb bed—I think I used up the last of what we had in the fridge."

She threw him a lighthearted wave and retraced her steps through the central lounge area, which they had come to call simply the Big Room. In redecorating, the Starbucks wanted most of all to keep the inn's early nineteenth-century charm intact. For the Big Room they had found braided rugs made in Nantucket, unbleached sprigged muslin curtains and slipcovers, and old-fashioned hurricane lamps. Flowers and magazines were ensconced in island-woven lightship baskets (which they had been lucky to find at an estate auction); and the walls were painted a serene pale olive, a color that seemed to be indigenous to Nantucket. On the mantelpiece above the cavernous stone fireplace were several fine examples of scrimshaw, that art of whalebone engraving originated, no doubt, by some lonely whaler bored with idleness during a year's-long voyage. Melissa loved the Big Room; it was unpretentious but warmly welcoming.

Highcliffe Inn was not a large hotel; it contained only sixteen guest rooms, and even those were not yet fully occupied. But it was still early in the season, and since the inn had been closed for six years, time was needed to lure former guests back and attract new ones. A slight frown of concern crossed Melissa's face as she saw Mrs. Blankenship at the desk with her baggage, obviously checking out. She had understood the woman would be staying another week. Mrs. Blankenship was engaged in animated conversation with Ellen as Melissa approached.

"No, of course not, Ellen, everything was charming. I have no complaints at all. In fact, I hope to be back later in the summer. But Marjorie has developed this quaint notion that I should be with her when she has the baby, and it *will* be my first grandchild. So I'm off to Kansas for a month or two." She smiled absently at Melissa, then checked her watch uneasily. "I only wish the cab would hurry. I must make that plane to New York in time to get my connecting flight."

Lissa walked to the broad windows overlooking Cliff Road. Indeed, a yellow cab had just pulled off the public road and was climbing the winding lane that led to the front entrance of the inn. Melissa turned back into the room.

"Here's your cab now, Mrs. Blankenship. I'll help you with your bags."

She picked up the larger two of the three pieces of matched blue luggage, then backed through the screen door, opening it with her derrière, since both her hands were full. As she turned to resume her forward progress, she suddenly encountered an immovable object that sent her reeling back against the screen. Blinking dazedly into the sunlight, she found her face only inches away from that of the tall bronzed man from the bicycle collision.

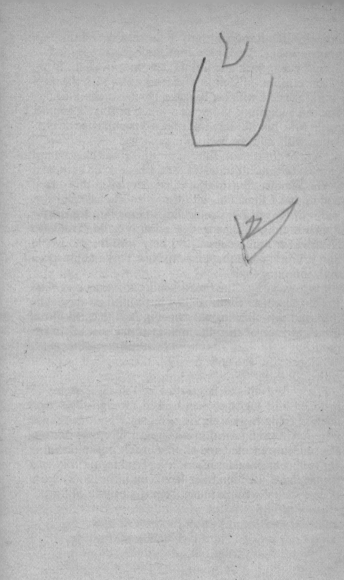

Chapter 2

"You!" Melissa was incredulous.

"I'm afraid so. Judging from the expression on your face, you would have preferred perhaps Frankenstein?"

She could not hide a tiny smile. He was outrageous, but the remark was humorous. He dropped his duffel bag on the floor of the porch, took Mrs. Blankenship's luggage from Melissa's hands, and, after a brief question as to its destination, hustled it into the trunk of the waiting cab. He turned with whirlwind efficiency, opened the back door for the lady, and closed her snugly inside. Then he wheeled once more to face Melissa.

"I guess this is small-world-department time. You're a guest here?" He seemed ingenuously surprised.

"Not exactly. My family runs the place."

"What a coincidence! I just asked the cabbie to take me to a nice place a bit out of the center of town, and we wind up here. Imagine that. It really *is* a small world, isn't it?"

His tone was one of naive wonderment, but Melissa thought she detected a glint of something more artful in his eyes. Suddenly aware that she was staring at him in a rather dazed way, she said almost crossly, "Well, if you want a room, come along and we'll get you registered."

He meekly followed her to the desk. Her mother was nowhere in sight, so Melissa found herself unwillingly in charge. She handed him a registration card and drummed her fingers lightly as he filled it out. For some reason she was edgy.

"There you are, madam." He handed the card back to her with a flourish. *Rodney Wilshire,* it read, and the name was followed by a New York address. He stood silently, watching her examine the card.

"Now that you know my name, may I know yours so we can consider ourselves formally introduced?"

"Melissa Starbuck." She reached for a room key, then turned again to face him. "Do you prefer a sea view or a view of the moors?"

"Oh? Moors, really? As in *Wuthering Heights?*" He raised an eyebrow with infuriating archness as Melissa nodded. "How nice to have a choice—"

"The rooms facing the moors are quieter," she stated flatly.

"Nevertheless I'll take the sea, I think."

There was something patronizing in his words. Melissa irritably jerked the key from its wall hook and instructed him to follow her. She led him up the broad mahogany stairs and down the cool uncarpeted hallway.

"Starbuck," he mused as she flung open a window to air the room. "With that name, you must be a native. On the way out I saw all sorts of Starbuck thises-and-thats."

"It's a well-known name in these parts, yes. My father was born here." She did not feel it necessary to inform him of her own off-islander status. This was only her second visit, and the first had been made more than ten years before. "I hope you'll be comfortable," she said, playing the role of professional innkeeper a bit self-consciously. "Lunch will be served from noon to two. We're on the European plan, as you probably noticed from the desk sign."

"Thank you, Miss Starbuck," he replied with grave formality.

She closed the door, feeling that she had somehow been bested in the verbal sparring. But there had really been no sparring . . . her feeling was ridiculous.

* * *

Melissa stayed busy during the lunch hour, helping Sally and her father refill the tureen of cold leek soup and the platter of sherried chicken. At Highcliffe Inn the guests ate family-style at four big round captain's tables. Unfortunately, only one of them was filled at present. Melissa looked at the almost empty dining room and had to remind herself again that the dearth of guests should not worry her—it was only early June and the season proper had not really started.

By a quarter after two the dining room had emptied of guests, and the Starbucks sat down to have their own meal. Lissa told her parents about the new guest and her early-morning run-in with him. "I suppose he didn't want lunch," she said, her mouth full of the fragrantly herbed chicken. "Maybe he had a late breakfast."

Rodney Wilshire suddenly appeared on the stairs and strode to their table. He had changed from his rather rumpled business suit into a pair of tan chinos and a loose white sweater.

"*Mea culpa,*" he said with what Melissa considered an ill-conceived attempt at humility. "I'm late, I know— must have fallen asleep on that superb bed. Are there, by any chance, any leftovers available to a malnourished but repentant culprit?" He bestowed a dazzling smile on Ellen. "I'm Rod Wilshire."

Before Melissa could launch into her explanation of why mealtimes had to be strictly adhered to (she had no intention of allowing her father to spend twenty-four hours a day in the kitchen), her mother leapt from her seat, motioning Rod Wilshire into the chair next to Melissa's. "Of course there's food left. I'll fix you a plate right away. Oh, I'm Ellen Starbuck. This is my husband, Paul, and I believe my daughter, Melissa, you've already met."

"In a manner of speaking," he replied, his eyes twinkling.

"Head-on. Twice." Melissa spoke dryly, noticing again that maddening twitch at the corners of his mouth. "Peo ple who don't look where they're going are a menace to society."

"Come, come, Miss Starbuck. I wasn't the one backing out the door or pedaling a bicycle at roughly the speed of light."

"I'll help Mother." Melissa addressed her father, pointedly ignoring Rod Wilshire, and abruptly left the table. How she wanted to flail out at him. He was disgustingly cocksure. But she could not be rude to a paying guest . . . not if this hotel venture was going to pay off for the Starbuck family. Biting her tongue in impotent ire, she flounced through the swinging doors into the kitchen.

Rod Wilshire smiled at Paul Starbuck ruefully. "I'm afraid I've got off on the wrong foot with your very lovely daughter."

Paul chuckled. "She inherited that temper from me. But we're alike in another way: it all blows over very quickly." He shifted his position as he took a sip of iced tea. "Having an early vacation, are you, Mr. Wilshire?"

"You might say that, yes." Rod's answer came only after a longish pause.

"How did you happen to choose Nantucket? I mean, most people think of this island as strictly a midsummer place, though it certainly has its own brand of charm during all four seasons."

Again there was a momentary hesitation. "A friend of mine has visited here several times. She's always loved it a lot, so I thought I should investigate it for myself."

"I see." Paul sensed in Rod Wilshire a reluctance to go into further detail, and at that moment their conversation was interrupted by the return of Ellen and Melissa to the dining room carrying overflowing dishes of food.

Rod attacked the meal with gusto. After a few mouthfuls he offered an apology for his voraciousness: "I haven't eaten in some hours. We flew in from Greece last night."

"Oh?" Ellen obviously found Mr. Wilshire highly interesting. "What were you doing in Greece?"

22

"My firm sent me there. We had thought the job would last for several months, but—" He paused and changed tack. "Well, to make a long story short, it ended sooner than we expected. But it was rather hectic while it lasted. In any case, here I am."

"Nantucket is a wonderful place to do nothing," Ellen observed. "If that's what you're of a mind to do," she amended hastily. "Otherwise, if you want golf, tennis, sailing, fishing, it's the perfect place for all those things, too."

Paul Starbuck eagerly rejoined the conversation at the mention of sailing. "But I'd better warn you if you're a novice sailor: the tides around the jetties at Brant Point are very strong. Try to take a Nantucketer with you the first couple of times you go out."

"Thanks for the tip. I'll keep that in mind." Rod got up from the table and bowed slightly to Ellen and Melissa. Since she had sat back down, Melissa had not said a word but had engaged herself busily with her apple cobbler. Now Rod, standing behind her, leaned over her shoulder and said in a low, confidential tone, "I hope our future meetings will not be quite so rich in drama as our first two, Miss Starbuck."

Lissa tossed her head and looked up at him briefly. "I couldn't agree more."

"The food was superlative. Thank you for taking pity on a starving man, Mrs. Starbuck."

Ellen laughed. "Oh, please. Informality is the keynote here. Make it Ellen and Melissa."

Rod glanced at Melissa, and she consented with an ungracious nod. He smiled at her disarmingly as Ellen added, "And by the way, you gave your compliments to the wrong chef. Paul does most of the cooking."

"Indeed?" Rod Wilshire arched an eyebrow. "Then my compliments to you, sir." He stifled a yawn. "Well, I believe jet lag has caught up with me. I feel in need of a siesta. Dinner is at—?"

23

"Six to eight," Melissa said curtly.

Rod nodded, then went upstairs, taking the steps two at a time.

Ellen Starbuck was enthusiastic. "He's a very charming man, isn't he?"

Paul Starbuck was uncharacteristically hesitant in answering. "There was something—oh, I don't know, I wouldn't want to use the word *evasive,* but—taciturn about him in talking about his—what he was doing in Greece. Odd."

"He also sounds like a male chauvinist," Melissa added.

Ellen looked puzzled. "Why on earth do you say that, Lissa?"

"Oh, he was so surprised that Dad did the cooking."

"Well, that's a rather flimsy reason for labeling him a male chauvinist, isn't it?" Ellen laughed her light, tinkling southern laugh.

Their postprandial conversation was interrupted by Doris. "Miss Ellen, room 305 wants to make a long-distance call, and when I tried, I must have been doing something wrong because he got cut off. Could you take over?"

Doris Emerson was Sally's daughter, a high-school senior who came in during meal hours to run the desk. Since she had had the job for only a week, she was not yet familiar with the more intricate workings of the switchboard.

Paul jumped to his feet. "I'll do it, hon," he said to his wife. "You haven't even had time to finish your lunch."

He went through the open archway that separated the dining area from the Big Room, and took over the call. He did not realize till he heard the voice that room 305 was the one in which Melissa had settled Rod Wilshire.

"Can I help you, Mr. Wilshire?"

"Is this Mr. Starbuck? Oh . . . yes . . . I was trying to call my firm in New York and there seems to be some difficulty on the line. Maybe you could put me through."

24

"I'll certainly have a go at it. We had a storm blow through a couple of days ago and the telephone lines have been a bit unpredictable since then."

Rod gave him the number and Paul Starbuck dialed it carefully, waiting to be sure the connection was clear. He did not catch the company name the New York receptionist laconically gave in answering. But when Rod Wilshire identified himself and asked for a Mr. Cookson, the secretary's attitude abruptly changed to one of eager alertness.

"Oh, yes, Mr. Wilshire, you're in charge of the Nantucket salvage operation. I know Mr. Cookson is very eager to hear from you. Just a moment."

Paul Starbuck hung up, a thoughtful frown furrowing his brow. Curious, he took Rod Wilshire's registration card from the file and read the firm's name: Oceanic Surveying, Inc.

He remained in deep thought as he traversed the lounge back into the dining room. *Oceanic Surveying. Nantucket salvage operation.* It was easy enough to put two and two together when one combined those phrases. Rod Wilshire was obviously on the island to try to do underwater salvaging from one or more of the wrecked ships that had foundered over the centuries on the treacherous surrounding shoals. Navigation around Nantucket was not for the fainthearted: the island sat small and alone in the vast Atlantic, exposed to sometimes brutal gales and thick blind fogs. More than one skillful and valorous sea captain had surrendered his ship to the wild sea there.

Paul Starbuck was not only an ardent sailor but also an ardent ecologist, and had been since long before the word became fashionable. The thought of an unscrupulous group of scavengers turning the brilliant dark blue Nantucket waters into a roiled and angry mud bed was anathema to his sea-loving soul inherited from generations of Starbuck whalemen and sailors.

One thing, however, puzzled him deeply. Most of the vessels strewn on the ocean bed around Nantucket carried no such exotic cargo as gold, silver, or precious stones. The vast majority had been laden with dry goods, cotton, or salt, none of which would have survived even a week of being waterlogged. Where, then, lay the profit in salvaging such ships?

Melissa noticed the unusual ruddiness of Paul Starbuck's face as he rejoined them at the table. "What's the matter, Dad?" It was obvious that something about the phone call from room 305 had upset her father. Rod Wilshire seemed to create havoc at every turn. It was almost laughable.

Paul sighed heavily. "Rod Wilshire seems to be a personable man," he said. "But I suspect he may spell trouble for Nantucket Island."

Chapter 3

"What do you mean, Paul?" Ellen's voice rose in surprise. "I thought Mr. Wilshire was the nicest thing that's happened to us yet."

Even Melissa, who was beginning to think of Rod Wilshire as an accident waiting to happen, was amazed at her father's ominous statement. "What's he done now?"

"I put through his call to New York and was waiting to be sure the connection was clear. The woman who answered the phone said something about a Nantucket salvage operation." He turned to Melissa: "When you checked him in, did you notice the company he was with?" Melissa shook her head blankly. "Well, he happens to be with something called Oceanic Surveying. Now that seems to be pretty conclusive evidence that Rod Wilshire is here to do salvaging in Nantucket waters. And if there's anything we don't need around here, it's a bunch of divers swarming all over the beaches and leaving a wake of flotsam and jetsam and creating general havoc. If we think business is bad now, just wait till Oceanic Surveying gets through with these beaches."

Ellen demurred gently. "But, Paul, don't they have to get permission from the state or township or someone to undertake an operation like that?"

But Paul Starbuck would not be calmed. "The State Marine Board, I think they call it, has to approve it, yes. But they're probably patsies when a big New York firm with plenty of money to throw around comes up here."

Even Melissa was a little taken aback by her father's vehemence and somewhat alarmed as to its possible physical effects on him. "Now wait a minute, Dad. I think you may be borrowing trouble. Not that I think Rodney Wilshire would be incapable of something like that. I don't trust that man an inch. But aren't you basing all this on a pretty flimsy supposition?"

Paul Starbuck looked at his only daughter fondly and smiled. She had always been able to calm him almost instantly. It was only when father and daughter were both angry at the same time that it was wise to give them a wide berth.

"Maybe you're right, Lissa. We'll just have to keep our eyes open and wait and see. In any case, we need all the paying guests we can get at the moment."

When Rod Wilshire appeared that night for dinner, every eye in the dining room was drawn to him as if magnetized. He wore a cream-colored dinner jacket with gray flannel trousers, and the effect was, to put it mildly, devastating. Melissa was helping her mother serve table and suddenly and irrationally felt dowdy in her white cotton peasant blouse and full apple-green skirt. Why hadn't she chosen something a little more sophisticated? Then she reproached herself for even having such a silly, shallow thought. Why should she care what Rod Wilshire thought of her, or even if he thought of her at all? She blushed furiously as she seated him and introduced him to the Traxons, an elderly couple traveling with their grandchildren. Major Traxon, a World War II veteran, and his wife had come to Nantucket with an eye to investing in a summer retirement cottage.

As Melissa served the broiled shrimp and avocado salad she caught snatches of their conversation. Mr. Traxon, a thin, balding, jolly man, was holding forth enthusiastically: "Yes, we went over to 'Sconset this afternoon and looked at a house there. I have an idea we might prefer

28

that to Nantucket Town. It has an unspoiled charm and relaxation that's just right for a couple of old fossils like Nettie and myself."

His wife, a rather coquettish white-haired woman who went to great pains to preserve her remaining traces of beauty, protested, "You speak for yourself, Major. I certainly never think of myself as an 'old fossil,' and I don't remember granting *you* permission to call me one." She smiled at Rod and lifted her chin flirtatiously. "I say youth is a state of mind."

Rod inclined his head in debonair agreement. "I think you're exactly right, Mrs. Traxon. And certainly you're a lovely example of that theory. But loveliness seems to be a common denominator among the Traxon women."

"There, you see?" Nettie crowed triumphantly to her husband. "There's only one old fossil in the Traxon family, and we all know who that is! Don't we, children?"

"Children" was perhaps a misnomer for the two young people with the Traxons. The boy, Jody, was about sixteen, and the girl, Janet, seventeen or eighteen. Melissa looked at Janet Traxon more closely. The Traxons had checked in only yesterday, and at that time Janet, in her plaid shirt and cutoff jeans, had looked like a child. Tonight, however, her brown hair was piled high, with enchanting tendrils carelessly fringing her forehead. She wore small pearl earrings and a pink linen dress and looked quite the young lady.

When Melissa went back into the kitchen, the door did not slam only because it was free-swinging and had nothing to slam against. Rod Wilshire was truly a disgusting creature. It was obvious he slathered his charm around like marmalade on bread. Grandmother or granddaughter —it made no difference to him.

Melissa casually sidled up to her father, who was dishing up sherbet cups of fresh strawberries in Chantilly cream. "By the way, when you were talking to Rod Wil-

29

shire this afternoon, did he happen to say how long he'll be staying?"

Paul Starbuck's concentration was all on the desserts, each of which he was garnishing with an especially large whole berry. "No, Lissa. The subject never came up. Why, honey?"

Melissa did not answer the question. "Are you ready for these desserts to go out now?"

"Yes, if you'll just get that green tray from the shelf. I think it'll hold them all."

The dinner over at last, the Starbucks sat down for their family meal. The guests had disappeared in a hurry. The sea air and the relaxed atmosphere seemed an invitation to call it a night early. Melissa, whose appetite was usually ravenous, picked at her food with such disinterest that her father finally asked if he had come a cropper with his new recipe for the shrimp.

"Oh, no, it's delicious. Too much of that apple cobbler at lunch, I guess."

Ellen gave her daughter a worried glance. "You'd better eat, Lissa. You're working awfully hard, you know—you have to keep up your strength."

"That's a switch"—Melissa chided her mother with a faint laugh. "You're usually telling me not to gobble so."

"I know, but that's the trouble with you, Lissa. You wouldn't know a happy medium if you met one in the middle of the road."

They all laughed then, and Paul changed the subject. "Lissa, did your mother tell you Benny's coming home in two weeks?"

"No!" Melissa exclaimed with delight. Her younger brother, Benny, had been in Vermont for the school year. A sixteen-year-old of superior intellect but extreme moodiness, Benny had spent the year at a progressive academy for the gifted, which his school counselor had recommended.

As children, Benny and Melissa had had some knock-down fights, but within the last several years Melissa had realized how very much she loved her brilliant introverted younger brother. The hoydenish Melissa was the daredevil of the two; Benny much preferred his books and yoga. He had become a devotee of the latter at the age of twelve and since then had practiced its meditation and exercises religiously. Astronomy was another of his interests.

Friends of the family always marveled that offspring of the same parents could be so opposite in appearance and temperament. Melissa was petite, fiery of hair and temper; Benny had the physique of a bean pole and the disposition of a rather bewildered lamb. Once Melissa had grown out of her childish urge to strangle him at least once a day, she had become downright doting and extremely protective of him.

Now she greeted the news of his imminent arrival with exuberant anticipation. "Exactly when will Benny be here?"

"A week from Saturday, I think," Ellen answered.

Paul Starbuck went into the kitchen to make out the menus for the following day, and Ellen went upstairs to select some new sheets she would purchase on her next visit off-island (many Nantucketers insisted on referring to the continental United States as America).

Melissa, vaguely restless, wandered out to the wide porch that ran the length of the old hotel. The bulbs in the new coachmen's lamps were too dim; she'd speak to Jason about it tomorrow. She looked out over the shrub-covered terrain, which fell away fairly steeply to the beach below. A light fog was rolling in from the sea, giving the normally panoramic view an air of unreality. She felt suddenly homesick for the hustle and bustle of the New York television studio—for the heady adrenaline high when the red eye of the camera lighted up; for the satisfaction when a scene had gone particularly well; for the evenings spent snuggled in her comfortable apartment while she pored over her lines for the following day. It was a hectic life but a wonderful one. In her present mood of nostalgia the sleepy early mornings, the pressure of time, the last-minute script changes, were all forgotten. She felt melancholic and somewhat isolated here on this point of land whose very name was the Indian word for *faraway*.

Impatient, she pulled herself out of her sentimental woolgathering and began to concentrate her thoughts on a renovation project the Starbucks were planning. They wanted to glass in one end of the open porch and use it as a dining deck during all but the coldest months. Melissa eyed the supporting columns and tried to estimate the distance between them. Tomorrow she would take an exact measurement and call Tribble's Hardware Store. Old Mr. Tribble had told her he could have the glass cut to order and delivered within a week or two.

Her thoughts were cut short by a sudden flash of light in the direction of the beach. Shading her eyes from the porch light and peering into the thickening fog, she could see nothing; the light had glimmered for only a fraction of a second. Then she heard a woman's voice in sharp emotional exclamation, whether of pleasure or alarm she could not tell. The pencil-slim beam of light flashed again, and she could hear the deeper resonance of a masculine voice join the feminine one. Melissa glanced hastily at her watch; it was after ten thirty. A night chill had set in with the fog; it was hardly the weather for a casual stroll along the beach.

She was about to call out when the beam of light appeared a third time, this time headed in the direction of the hotel. Melissa was standing on the extreme end of the porch where the light was dimmest; in the fog she must have been quite invisible. Some instinct kept her there, motionless. The light was moving erratically, as though held by someone under stress. Within a few seconds, as the voices came nearer and nearer, she could make out two faint figures, one carrying the other. As they approached,

32

she saw that it was Rod Wilshire with Janet Traxon in his arms.

Overcome by a confusing and illogical feeling that she was eavesdropping on a private moment, she shrank more deeply into the corner against the gray shingles until Rod Wilshire had opened the door and taken his burden inside.

Melissa lay awake for what seemed hours, and the longer she lay awake, the more furious she became. First of all, where were Janet Traxon's grandparents and why were they allowing her to run wild on the beach? The child must still be a minor in spite of her grown-up airs. Janet herself was extremely foolish to be out in the middle of the night with someone who was practically old enough to be her father. The most explosive fury of all, however, was reserved for Rod Wilshire. Talk about irresponsibility! It was obvious the man had no sense of decency whatever, to respond to a mere slip of a girl whom he had met only that evening. And he had flirted with the child's grandmother with equal audacity. He was beyond the pale.

The next morning Melissa was on the phone with Mr. Tribble when Rod Wilshire passed through the Big Room on his way out. He was wearing a pair of well-worn jeans and a light blue Windbreaker. When he saw Melissa, he gave her a light, mocking version of a courtly bow. Everything he did was so exaggerated, she thought in disgust. Surely a simple good-morning would have been sufficient!

She sighed and hung up. She would have to bike in to Tribble's—there were too many choices to make: thicknesses, grades, and tints of glass; wooden, aluminum, or steel frames; French-door or casement openings. It was much too complex to settle over the telephone.

She ran upstairs for a sun hat. She was one of the few fortunate redheads able to tan without dire results, but the producer of her show had warned her not to come back with a tan, since, within the context of the program, her character was away in prison. As she passed the elder

Traxons' room she heard the major's voice raised in argument.

". . . and I say we should move out today. We know that little motel in 'Sconset can take us."

"But, dear, what's really happened that's so awful? Janet sneaked out of her room and sprained her ankle, that's all."

"And was delivered to our door by that shifty-eyed adventurer. I knew the minute I laid eyes on him, you can't trust that man."

"You're just being unreasonable. It's a good thing he was there—you wouldn't have wanted Janet to spend all night hurt and alone, would you?"

"My God, woman, if *he* hadn't been there, *she* wouldn't have been there! Can't you see—"

Melissa broke into a run. She did not want to hear any more. But what she had overheard only proved her conjectures about the character of Rod Wilshire.

In town she had a lengthy but delightful conference with Mr. Tribble about the glassed-in deck. He was a native islander approaching his eightieth birthday, he said proudly. Melissa was genuinely surprised; he looked sixty-ish. Once their business matters were wrapped up, he sensed Melissa was a willing audience, and began spinning tales he had heard from his father and grandfather, who in turn had heard them from theirs. He told her about the decline and final death throes of the whaling industry when petroleum was discovered and whale oil became suddenly obsolete. He told her about the great fire of 1846, when a third of Nantucket Town was reduced to ashes. Following that catastrophe, which left the entire island economically devastated, many able-bodied young men were lured three thousand miles across the continent to seek fame and fortune in the California gold rush of 1849.

He confided that he'd been employed by the Coast Guard as a revenuer during Prohibition. European ships, laden with Scotch whisky or French champagne, would anchor a few miles offshore and be met by smaller boats that would then take on the contraband liquor and deliver it to Boston or Long Island Sound.

"Well, one night we caught a boat right in the act. Our running lights were off, and they had no idea we were within a million miles. They loaded up with maybe a hundred cases. But before they could get under way, we stationed our boat—which was a damn sight bigger and tougher than theirs—right in front of them. They had no choice but to stop. We boarded and took them in custody. But the thing I couldn't get over was, the head scalawag of those rumrunners was my *next-door neighbor.*"

"What happened? Did he go to jail?"

"Yep, he did. For a year. But I didn't testify agin him. There were plenty of others that could do that. Down the years I've often wondered what I would have done if I'd been the only witness who could have put him away. Well, he was doing something illegal, no doubt about it. But I don't believe I could have sent that man to jail. He saved my boy's life one time when the boy swam out too far and nearly drowned. No sir, I don't believe I coulda been the one to send that man to jail."

Biking back home, Melissa pondered the moral dilemma posed by Mr. Tribble's story. When personal loyalty clashed with technical obeisance to the law, where did one's moral duty lie? It was a question that gnawed and intrigued. When she came out of her reverie and glanced at her watch, she realized she would be late getting back to Highcliffe to help with lunch. But the old man's stories had held her spellbound, and she began to feel the tug of possessive pride that binds so many to the fiercely independent, cantankerous island.

Once she reached the hotel, she muttered her apologies and pitched in at once. But her assistance was not really needed—there were only three guests in the room.

After the three had complimented Paul Starbuck on the

35

savory quahog chowder and bacon quiche and left the room, Melissa sank into her place at the table. "Where is everybody today, anyway?" she asked, curious.

Paul and Ellen Starbuck exchanged a brief glance, and Ellen answered, her southern drawl more hesitant than usual: "Mr. Wilshire told me this morning he wouldn't be back in time for lunch, and I suppose that's just as well. The Traxons apparently thought their granddaughter wasn't safe in the same hotel with him, and they're gone for good. They checked out this morning around ten."

Chapter 4

Late spring drifted imperceptibly into early summer. The tulips and daffodils gave way to ever more flamboyant displays of the rambling red roses that were almost as much a Nantucket trademark as the ubiquitous gray cedar shingles. In the fields the perennial glossy green of the holly and bayberry seemed to become richer; in shaded bogs the swamp maples, tupelos, and ferns put forth shy, inquiring chartreuse buds. Even on the palisade between Highcliffe Inn and the sea the beach plum and wintergreen bushes appeared to take new life from the steadily moderating southern winds.

From the day Mr. Tribble had held her enthralled with his yarns of derring-do among the hardy early settlers, Melissa had made it a habit to stop by the Atheneum Library when she went into town. The building itself inspired her. Built in 1847, its gleaming white Ionic columns rose as a symbol of order and stability. Miss Harding, the pretty blond librarian, was unfailingly generous with her time and expertise. Melissa would check out two or three books; and most nights, absorbed in tales of the awesome hardships endured by the whalers and marveling at their incredible stamina and spirit, she would read herself to sleep. But her reading sessions were not long ones; her days were busy from dawn until the last dinner dish was cleared, and usually within a few minutes she found her eyelids closing and her weary body demanding sleep.

She had seen little of Rod Wilshire in the two weeks

since he had checked in. He had rented a small car and spent most of each day away. He seemed to have settled in for a good long stay; a small trunk shipped from New York had been delivered to his room. Since the incident with Janet Traxon he had distinguished himself mainly by his absence. Although he had implied to her father that he had come to Nantucket for a rest, his clothes were not those of the ordinary vacationer. He dressed habitually in functional tan or blue chinos topped by a denim work shirt or a white hooded athlete's sweat shirt. He was usually out even before the Starbucks arose to prepare breakfast.

By late June the trickle of guests had become, if not a flood, at least a small but steady stream. While it was gratifying to see the visitors enjoying Paul Starbuck's superb meals, it meant more work for everyone. In addition to Sally Emerson and Marie in the kitchen and Sally's daughter, Doris, part-time on the desk, a new chambermaid had been hired to dust and clean the rooms. The inn was not yet in the black, but it was Paul's theory that tireless effort would eventually put it there. Melissa's attempts at slowing her father down were not always successful.

One night when the dinner guests had been particularly demanding, Melissa shooed both her parents upstairs before nine, promising that she would oversee the kitchen cleanup and close the downstairs windows for the night. As in most public houses on Nantucket, the doors were never locked and the windows were closed only as protection against a sudden squall. There had recently been a few rumors of minor vandalism downtown, but the Cliffside area was so far untroubled by such problems.

Lissa had bade Sally and Marie good night and was now trying to cope with an especially balky window in the Big Room. A whisper of damp fog floated in. She thought she could hear through the open window, very distantly, the Lisbon bell in the tower of Old South Church announcing the nine-o'clock curfew with its customary fifty-two rings.

The reason for that particular number had been lost to history, but it had become an entrenched tradition.

She started at the sudden sound of a voice very close behind her: "May I be of some help?"

She recognized the amused, sardonic tone at once: Rod Wilshire. She was all the more surprised because he had not appeared at meals for the last two days. But she relinquished the chore without argument and even with a sense of relief. Running Highcliffe Inn must have taken its toll on her, too, these past few days, she thought ruefully. Rod strode to the window purposefully and slammed it shut.

He turned to face her with a sudden grin. "Anything else you need a man to turn his hand to?"

"I could have closed the window myself," she said, instantly on the defensive. "I had just hit my fingernail on the sash and stopped to see if I had broken it."

"I'm sure." He maintained a gravely respectful air.

"I thought you had deserted Highcliffe Inn for other parts." Her confusion over blurting out such a foolish statement was compounded by his knowing grin. "I mean, I haven't happened to see you around lately."

"Had to go in to New York," he answered briefly. "Just got back."

"But—" She knew no ferries were due in from the mainland at this hour.

He anticipated the question. "Flew back. The plane was delayed because of fog over the sound."

She looked at him more closely. He too looked a bit weary. An intuitive question sprang to her lips. "Would you like a cup of coffee?"

A faint version of the lopsided grin appeared. "You bet. I sure would."

He followed her through the swinging doors into the spotless kitchen. She had turned off the low flame under the blue enamel percolator just minutes before—the coffee only needed heating up. She relighted the jet and came back to the butcher-block table where he sat. For once, his habit of worldly one-upmanship had deserted him. His shoulders sagged; he looked dispirited.

They sipped coffee in silence for a moment before he spoke, and when he did, his voice was uncharacteristically meek. "Are there any cold cuts around I could make a sandwich out of?"

Melissa looked at him, pondering the simple question. "Oh. Yes, of course. You didn't have dinner?"

"No," he admitted. "My dinner plans were—changed at the last minute."

"How about some bacon and eggs?" she asked impulsively. "Wouldn't that be nicer than a cold sandwich?"

"To tell you the truth, I can't think of anything in the world I'd like better."

Inspired by his obvious anticipation, Melissa turned the bacon to the peak of crispness, carefully babied the eggs until the whites were firm and the yolks creamy, and buttered three thick slices of homemade bread. She found a jar of Sally's wild plum preserves, put up last summer, and sat down again with her coffee. She watched him clean the plate in what seemed seconds.

He touched his napkin to his lips and looked up from the empty plate sheepishly. "It seems to me I'm always apologizing for my gluttony."

She shrugged off the self-denigrating remark. "I'm glad you enjoyed it. Most people get so spoiled by my father's cooking that my efforts seem amateurish by comparison."

She had rinsed his plate and had reached out to clear the coffee cups when he said, "Melissa, if there's any coffee left, I'd love to have you join me in another cup."

She was about to tell him there was no more—after all, she had firmly decided that Rod Wilshire was no more than a conceited adventurer—but something in his eyes stopped the refusal before she could voice it. She poured the two coffees and reseated herself opposite him. Outside, the wind whistled faintly, and the kitchen, still warm from the day's cooking, seemed snug and comfy.

He toyed with his coffee cup for a moment. "I wanted to clear up something I think you may have misunderstood. . . ."

"You mean the accident with the bicycle? I'd forgotten about that long ago. You may even have been right—about my speeding, I mean—"

"No, no, I wasn't talking about that. Although I will say parenthetically that I *was* right about your speeding." The twinkle reappeared for a split second, then his face sobered again. "No, the thing with the Traxon girl. You see, I saw you at the end of the porch when I brought her in. At the moment I didn't have time to do anything about it—I didn't know how badly she was hurt, and I wanted to get her in to her grandparents as soon as possible."

Melissa interrupted him haughtily. "You don't have to go into all this. It's none of my business."

He overrode her interruption. "Oh, yes, it is. It's your business as well as your mother's and father's. I know the Traxons checked out the next day, and I got the feeling that I was the reason for that. So I think the whole situation may have been misread." She started to protest again, but he held up a palm to silence her. "I wasn't responsible for her being on the beach. I mean, I didn't invite her out for a walk. I was walking down the beach alone and she was suddenly there. I told her she'd better get back inside —she wasn't dressed for the night air—and she started back up the cliff, yelling to me that she'd race me up the hill. It was then she fell and hurt her ankle. That's the whole story."

"That's why those steps were roped off—to keep people away from them." Melissa's temper flared. "We might have been sued, you know, and—"

"Wait a minute! You've got a king-sized temper for such a tiny mite." Melissa bridled, but he plowed ahead: "You explode like a Roman candle. I knew from the first day I saw you, you'd be some kind of handful. I suppose that's why I—"

He stopped abruptly. Melissa's curiosity was irresistibly piqued. "Why you what?"

He paused, then confessed: "—told that little white lie about how I came to wind up at Highcliffe Inn."

"You mean it wasn't accidental? I thought the cab driver just happened to bring you here."

"That's what I wanted you to think. Actually, finding out where you belonged cost me the price of a dozen apples."

She frowned quizzically. "I don't follow."

"Well, you said something that morning about getting the avocados for the guests. My fantastic powers of deduction led me to conclude you must be connected with one of the hotels or inns. The plastic bag the avocados tumbled out of said Walter's Fresh Produce. I don't know how that happened to stick in my mind, but it did. So I tracked down the Walter's Fresh Produce place, then, with the purchase of a dozen apples, bribed Walter into telling me the identity of the smashing little redhead who had been in earlier in the day in search of avocados. Simple, my dear Watson." He leaned back in his chair, looking extraordinarily pleased with himself. The food and coffee had apparently resuscitated his sense of mischief.

Melissa reviewed his story. She could not help but be flattered that he had gone to such lengths to find her. But his conduct was still suspect in the Traxon episode. "That's all very nice, and I admire your ability as a master sleuth, but back to Janet Traxon for a—"

"Oh, yes. Back to that again, are we? Well, what else do you want to know?"

"I was saying that a supposedly adult man should have known better than to use those steps—"

"But, my dear little bundle of TNT, I didn't use them. I walked down the lane east of the beach when I went out, and was going to come back up the same way when Little Miss Traxon forcibly changed my plans by wrenching her ankle."

42

"All right, all right." Melissa was tired of discussing it. His answer sounded logical, and maybe it was. In any case, she'd probably never know. She was ready for the privacy of her own room and a good night's sleep. She felt tired and confused.

She reached again for the cups, but he took them from her hands and carried them to the sink. He turned on the faucet and gave a sudden yelp. "Holy—what are you trying to do, scald me to death? This water is hotter than the devil's own!"

"I'm sorry," she murmured sweetly. "If you hadn't been so hell-bent on getting those cups washed, I would have warned you." She pushed the swinging door into the Big Room and held it open somewhat impatiently. It had been a long day.

He started to follow her through, and as his hand reached out to keep the door from swinging shut, his fingers touched hers. His hard brown hand closed over hers suddenly and tightly, and Melissa felt an electric tingle suffuse her body with such intensity that she was held immobile in the doorway. Her eyes darted uncertainly to his face; his expression was one of naked longing. She felt hypnotized, suddenly bereft of her will.

Wordless, he led her through the Big Room and onto the porch that overlooked Nantucket Sound, closing the screen door noiselessly behind him. They stood together for a moment as the thickening mist enclosed them in a universe of their own. With a liquid movement, almost feline, Rod pulled her down into one of the chairs. In spite of the dampness of the evening fog Melissa felt as though she had developed a sudden inexplicable temperature. She brushed a hand across her forehead and found it unnaturally warm. Rod's arms were around her waist. Involuntarily her arm reached across his body to his shoulder. She could feel the tough, sinewed muscles beneath the thin shirt. His body, too, seemed slightly fevered.

His right arm moved from her waist to the back of her

neck, and slowly he turned her face to meet his. In the dim, haloed light of the coachmen's lamps she could see only his eyes, glittering darkly. His touch on her neck was weightless as a feather, yet she sensed a steely strength in his fingers. He increased the pressure of his forefinger, forcing her head ever closer to his own. And suddenly there was the throbbing of his mouth against hers, exploring, eliciting, demanding. She found herself responding fervently—a giddy natural force within her made any other reaction impossible. His urgency softened as he moved slightly away, and his tongue playfully traced the outline of her lips. She desperately wanted their mouths commingled again, and she offered him her parted lips. But instead he moved his head slowly and softly to her ear, and his tongue probed delicately and sensually inside. He caught her hand, brought it to his mouth, and began to lick her palm with swift playful laps.

Melissa thought wildly that she should extricate herself from this madness, but his hand squeezed hers for an instant, dropped it into her lap, and moved to her breast. He cupped the roundness with a touch so light she was not sure where his touch ended and her imagination began. She felt her nipples rise into tiny hardened peaks. Rational thought was beyond her.

Quite sharply his hand dropped away to the arm of the chair. Putting his hands under her elbows, he slowly forced her into a standing position and stood up beside her. "You'll catch cold," he said gruffly. "Let's go in."

He did not wait for her but led the way, holding the door open stiffly as she entered the lounge. He preceded her up the stairs, leaving her to follow in the dim night light as best she could. As they reached the second-floor landing, the floor on which the Starbucks maintained their private quarters, he turned briefly, his hand on the railing of the stairway that continued to the third floor. "I'm sorry, Melissa." His voice was scratchy, almost inaudible.

44

"My mistake." He wheeled abruptly and bounded up the final flight of stairs, almost as if he were being pursued.

She was left on the landing feeling like an abandoned fool who fully deserved her fate. She had cooked a hot meal for him, she had accepted his suspicious version of the escapade with Janet Traxon, she had been openly receptive to his sudden advances, and she had been instantly deserted without explanation. Her impulsiveness had led her into a humiliating rejection.

She let herself into her room, being careful to close the door noiselessly. Her parents slept two doors down, their room separated from hers only by a common sitting room. Above all, she did not want to disturb her father's rest.

By the time she crawled out of her clothes, leaving them strewn on the floor, she had talked herself into viewing the whole distasteful affair philosophically. There must be a sadistic streak in Rod Wilshire, she decided. *He must be one of those men who has to prove to himself that he can attract a woman; and when he has succeeded, his interest vanishes.* And how quickly and naively she had succumbed to his infantile game playing!

But never mind. She had learned her lesson and escaped relatively unscathed. Her last waking thought was a resolve never to forget in future the old adage about a burnt child avoiding the fire.

Chapter 5

Although Melissa had slept only fitfully, she found herself awake before six the next morning and went downstairs to make coffee. Surprisingly, her father was there before her.

"Dad! What in heaven's name are you doing up so early?"

"I might ask the same question of you, young lady."

"I dunno. Couldn't sleep. Thought I'd come down and have a pot of hot coffee waiting for you and Mother."

"Well, I've beat you to it. Help yourself."

When she returned to the table with her coffee, she noticed her father was poring with great concentration over some figures on the sheet of paper before him. As she sat down he looked up at her absent-mindedly and smiled.

"Looks like Highcliffe Inn is on the road to solvency, babe."

"How so?"

"Got a reservation yesterday for four people who'll be staying through the summer."

"But, Dad, that's just super! Why didn't you tell me right away?"

"Last night's dinner was so hectic, I didn't have time to think of anything else."

"When are they coming in?"

"Sunday afternoon."

"Gee," she mused, "then we're going to have our hands full over the weekend getting things ready for them, aren't we?" It was already Friday.

"You don't know the half of it, with Benny coming in too."

"Is it this weekend?" Her brother's arrival had completely slipped her mind.

"Indeed." He put his papers away and rose. "I'd better start breakfast." He paused and examined Melissa more closely. It wasn't like her to forget about Benny. "You feeling okay this morning, honey?"

She smiled up at him, attempting fo feign a degree of cheeriness. "Of course, Dad. Great."

He accepted her statement and began bustling about the stainless-steel and butcher-block room preparing the strawberry crêpes for the morning meal. Melissa welcomed the news of the four new arrivals not only out of financial considerations: it would keep her hands busy and her mind occupied. She ached with humiliation every time she thought of the previous evening's encounter with Rod Wilshire. One question spun round and round in her brain: Why? Why had he turned and deserted her so suddenly?

At nine o'clock she took her place at the registration desk—her mother had driven to 'Sconset in the Volkswagen for fresh clams. After breakfast was over, the Big Room was very quiet; most of the guests had left the inn for a day of fishing, tennis, or sight-seeing. Melissa was deep in one of her Nantucket histories, this one the incredible story of the great bank robbery of 1795 when political and religious prejudices led to the imprisonment of one Randall Rice, a hapless innocent, even though one of the three robbers had actually confessed!

Her concentration was shattered by the ring of the telephone. The nasal voice of the operator announced that there was a person-to-person call for Mr. Rodney Wilshire.

"Just a moment," Melissa said. "I'll ring his room."

There was no answer, which Melissa reported to the waiting operator. The operator spoke to someone, and

48

through the slight static of the connection Melissa heard a woman issue imperious instructions: "Please have him call Tracy Nightingale as soon as he returns. Tell him it's about last night's meeting." She followed the order with a number, which the operator repeated to Melissa. Melissa wrote down the message with a dull sinking in her heart and then put it in Rod's mailbox.

It was not until she sat back down and tried to resume her reading that she realized she was inordinately upset. The page swam before her eyes, and the words echoed and reechoed: "Tell him it's about last night's meeting."

As if the situation weren't already damaging enough to her self-esteem, Rod Wilshire had made his brief and aborted pass at her within a few hours of leaving another woman. Since he was a guest at Highcliffe, she would have to be at least civil to him, but even that would call for great self-control on her part. She only hoped she could restrain her temper on those occasions when contact with him was unavoidable.

He appeared unexpectedly for lunch; he had not been present for the midday meal in days. Doris Emerson was on the desk when he breezed into the Big Room whistling. Melissa was fussing with a massive arrangement of bearberry leaves which was to cover the open fireplace during the summer months.

She heard Doris call to him as he passed, telling him that he had a message.

After a few seconds' pause he asked the girl, "What time did this come in?"

"I don't know, Mr. Wilshire. I wasn't on duty yet. I believe Miss Melissa took it."

Melissa kept her head low, hoping the luxuriant foliage would conceal her whereabouts. But within a few seconds she heard his voice above her.

"You took this message, Melissa?"

She could feel her cheeks grow warmer until she knew her entire face was scarlet. At last she raised her eyes to

49

his. "Yes." She struggled to keep her voice even. "I'm sorry I forgot to list the time. It came in around ten thirty."

He frowned, then nodded. "Oh, by the way, I believe I'll have to be away for the weekend."

She was tempted to answer with a biting retort about how little his plans meant to her, but she merely nodded, her burning face buried in the leaves. He stood for a moment, then turned on his heel and bounded up the stairs. When Melissa passed the desk a few minutes later, she could see the switchboard light for room 305 blinking red. Presumably he was returning the call to Miss Nightingale. She wanted to ask Doris if that was indeed the case, but she reminded herself it was really none of her business.

After lunch she strolled toward the beach. Jason and his cohorts were finishing up the repair job on the beach steps, hauling away the last remnants of lumber and tools.

"Are they going to be painted, Jason?" she asked of the hefty bearded workman.

"Oh, yes, ma'am. This afternoon we'll give 'em a coat of protective sealer and do the final coat tomorrow morning. We'll do that before we put up the lights."

"Lights?"

"Yep. We're stringing a row of colored lights along the beach."

Melissa remembered her father had mentioned the idea a few days ago. She nodded as the men disappeared toward the rear of the building. The steps now offered easy access to the beach. The day was extraordinarily warm, and the breeze that sprang from the sea felt midsummerish. As a rule, it was not until July that summer really arrived at the island.

The colored lights would make a fairyland of the strip of sand, she thought. The guests' beach activities hereafter would not have to be confined to daylight hours. They could have barbecues, picnics, clambakes after dark. She snapped her fingers in sudden inspiration. Since the

50

weather was so beautifully balmy, since Benny was coming home, and since four guests were arriving who would be at Highcliffe for the whole season, why not celebrate the occasion by giving them a taste of Nantucket hospitality at its very finest? Rod Wilshire's unsettling presence would not be a problem, and the evening would be thoroughly casual and relaxing.

With great excitement she ran back up the palisade. Entering the kitchen, she blurted out, "Dad, I have an inspiration. Let's have a clambake!"

Paul looked up from the chopping board and shook his head with a resigned grin. "You're like a drop of mercury, Melissa, me girl. This morning you looked like you'd lost your last and very best friend. Now you're like a kid who's just discovered Christmas. A clambake, eh? Well, sure. I hope we'll have several before the summer's over—"

"But I mean this weekend. This Sunday night! The steps will be painted tomorrow, and the colored lights put up. Benny will be here, those new people—didn't you say they're coming in Sunday afternoon? It'll be the perfect time to sort of open the season officially."

"Melissa," he remonstrated weakly. He was trying to serve as a restraining influence, though it was not a role that came easily to him; he was by nature as impulsive as his daughter. "You've already said we're going to have our hands full—"

"I'll plan it all, Dad, truly. I'll do the shopping and the fire building and everything."

He cocked an eyebrow. "And what do you know about real Nantucket clambakes, you coof?" he asked, jokingly using the derogatory term by which the natives referred to off-islander aliens.

"Jason knows all there is to know. He'll tell me how to do everything; he told me the other day he would. I've been reading up. I know quite a lot myself."

Paul Starbuck gave in to her unquenchable enthusiasm

without much of a struggle. "All right. But remember, it's your party."

Melissa's mother had made another trip to 'Sconset for steamer clams and lobsters, and Melissa drove downtown on Saturday afternoon to meet Benny and to pick up fresh green peas and potatoes, the latter to be roasted in the beach fire. Corn on the cob was traditional, but it was too early in the season for that; the potatoes would be an acceptable substitute. The only thing to be cooked indoors would be the chowder. —

Melissa stopped off at the library to return some books, but the locked door reminded her it was closed on Saturday afternoon. She was about to leave when a slight sound from inside caught her ear, and at that moment the door opened and Miss Harding emerged.

"I'm sorry. I know this is an imposition—I know you're supposed to be closed, Miss Harding, but—"

"Melissa, please. No, it's quite all right. You only want to return these, don't you? I can take them. Be glad to."

"Thanks. That's awfully nice of you." Melissa handed her the books. "Goodness," she said as an afterthought, "do you work seven days a week?"

Amelia Harding laughed and shook her head. Most assuredly not the stereotypical librarian, she was extremely attractive and probably not yet thirty. Melissa had not had time to make friends with anyone remotely her contemporary, and now a brainstorm struck. "We're going to have a clambake on Sunday night. Would you like to join us?"

Amelia Harding looked somewhat taken aback. She knew that Melissa and her parents had taken over Highcliffe Inn, and she had briefly met both Paul and Ellen. But she was hesitant about accepting such an impromptu invitation. Melissa sensed her reluctance and intensified her persuasiveness.

"Please do. You'd enjoy it. It's all going to be very

casual and spur-of-the-moment. We didn't even start thinking about it till yesterday, but it just all of a sudden seemed a great idea."

"Well, perhaps I could. This is my busy season, and it seems sometimes my nose must surely bear the imprint of a grindstone. I could use a little relaxation."

Melissa laughed. "Terrific. Come out about five, then, all right?" She waved good-bye and went to Steamboat Wharf to meet Benny's ferry. The passengers were streaming down the ramp as she drove up, but she did not see her brother among them. When the thin teen-ager in dark glasses stopped by the side of her car, she assumed he wanted to ask directions.

"Well, sis," he called through the window, "aren't you going to unlock the door and let me in?"

"Benny?" She looked at him again. He seemed to have grown much taller and even thinner. He threw his luggage on the backseat, then leaned over and kissed her. She began the drive home. "I thought they might have fattened you up a little," she said lightly, "but no such luck, I see."

"Oh, no, not you. I expected to hear that from the elder members of the family, but I thought you at least would have the decency to desist."

She half smiled. Benny's slightly stilted precociousness with words had not changed. "Aren't you eating anymore?"

A groan preceded his answer. "I'm eating like the proverbial swine, and I'll prove it to you as soon as I can find nourishment to masticate within my mandibles."

Melissa's worry subsided. Perhaps it was only his metabolism that kept him so skinny. "Tomorrow night we're having a big clambake, mostly in your honor. But I told Dad I'd do most of the work, and I'm enlisting you as my first mate."

"Is that any way to treat a guest of honor?" he grumbled good-naturedly.

Melissa laughed and turned onto the private lane up to the hotel, where Paul and Ellen were waiting on the porch to greet the youngest Starbuck.

True to her promise, Melissa kept Benny running all day Sunday. In the morning they took the lifeguard boat and went out in search of seaweed. Paul had warned them to stay close to shore and away from the current of the jetties. So they headed toward Dionis Beach and, within a couple of hours, had the boat piled so high with the slimy dark brown substance they had to tow it by swimming ahead of it. Melissa reveled in the shock of the still-icy water; it jolted her alive. They collected driftwood along the beach and gathered rocks the size of ostrich eggs. Then they made a bonfire of the driftwood with the rocks beneath.

In the late afternoon they dug a shallow pit in the sand and raked the rocks into it. A layer of seaweed would keep the shellfish and potatoes insulated from the intense heat of the rocks so the roasting process could be suitably slow. Benny worked willingly and hard throughout the day. They were so intent on their labors there was not much time for conversation about his year at school or her life in New York.

They brought out big folding tables, spread them with red-checked cloths, arranged the paper plates and chowder cups, and now all was ready for the guests.

Melissa went upstairs to shower and change. Her excitement grew with every moment; it was the inn's first real social occasion. She took out a pair of flowered green pants and tied a yellow shirt midriff-style. Her mood of anticipation was tinged with revenge. She supposed it was petty, but it was a source of satisfaction that Rod Wilshire would not be around for the fun. Life was so much simpler without him. She would have a chance to play catch-up with Benny and to chat with the new guests with some degree of poise and serenity. She would not have to spend what should be a carefree evening trying to avoid making awkward conversation with Rod.

When she skipped down the beach steps and onto the sand, she was surprised to find the new guests already assembled. Her father was serving them large paper cups of beer from the keg that stood near the tables. She must have spent more time in dressing than she'd thought. She approached her father in some embarrassment.

"I'll do that, Dad. Remember our bargain? I'm to do the work and you're to enjoy yourself."

He introduced her to the new guests, and it occurred to her for the first time that they were all male. She supposed she had subconsciously assumed they would be two couples.

"And this is Mr. Hylton," Paul said in conclusion. The other names were a jumble to her, for she was concentrating on the peculiar expression on her father's face and trying to fathom the reason for it. Things became much clearer with his next sentence: "Our new guests, it seems, Melissa, are all affiliated with Oceanic Surveying." For a fraction of a second he must have taken her astonishment for incomprehension, for he amplified his statement: "Oceanic Surveying, you remember? Mr. Wilshire's salvaging company."

His emphasis on the word *salvaging* was so slight that no one but Melissa would have noticed it. But she caught at once the disapproval with which her father spoke the word.

Uh oh, she thought, *looks like it's going to be a bumpy night.*

Chapter 6

The varicolored lights and the crackling, leaping flames cast an enchanted glow on the strip of beach. Melissa had brought out miniature versions of the Big Room's hurricane lamps and scattered them on the long table where the lighted tapers, even though protected by the glass cylinders, danced in the wind from the sea. The sound of the surf rose and fell in the distance. Occasionally lights from a passing freighter or fishing boat would bob briefly on the far horizon, like fireflies in the night, then silently disappear.

Though Melissa and Benny tried to keep Paul Starbuck from physical exertion, he insisted on periodically moving aside the wet covering tarpaulin to check the progress of the food. When the shellfish was uncovered, its mouthwatering briny aroma filled the night. Paul seemed in a jovial mood; he had apparently decided to forget his concern about the men from Oceanic Surveying, at least until the social occasion was over.

When the party had been under way for perhaps half an hour, Melissa heard the scrape of automobile tires on the gravel drive leading to the inn and went up to discover that Amelia Harding had arrived. But she was not alone.

"Melissa, my car refused to function tonight, and Trish, who lives across the hall from me, was kind enough to bring me out. Trish Lessing, Melissa Starbuck."

Melissa examined the unexpected guest with friendly interest. She was a tall, slender brunette wearing a dark red flower-splashed caftan. Although its lines were flowing, the fabric was so soft that it clung to her figure seductively.

"You're sure you'll be able to get a ride home later, Amelia?" Trish asked, preparing to drive away.

Melissa protested at once. "Oh, no, you've got to stay! We have four new men who checked in this afternoon. I'm sure they'd welcome feminine companionship."

Trish hesitated. "I really shouldn't—I was just getting ready to wash my hair when Amelia knocked on my door. I'm not even dressed for a beach party."

"You look wonderful," Melissa said, and meant it. Trish's long black hair flowed exotically down her back; she might almost have been transplanted from a South Seas island.

Amelia joined in. "Do stay, Trish. You've been working awfully hard for a nineteen-year-old. Come on."

The three of them made their way down the beach steps, and Melissa introduced the new arrivals to the others, laboriously sorting out the four men from Oceanic. There was Lester Hylton, a shy blond; Bob Converse, a bearded wiry man of perhaps forty; and two brothers, Jim and Jerry Wilson, both in their early twenties. They all had the muscular, well-tuned look of superb athletes, which Melissa supposed was a necessity for deep-sea divers. The word *divers* reminded her what they were here for: to plunder the sea that even now alternately sighed and rumbled around them.

Jerry Wilson seemed to be quite taken with Trish Lessing; he followed her around with a glazed look in his eyes, lighting her frequent cigarettes and replenishing her beer. Amelia Harding was talking animatedly to Bob Converse and Ellen. Only Benny seemed to be at loose ends; he walked along the shore dragging in a few more gnarled branches of driftwood, but he seemed preoccupied and ill at ease.

"Having a good time, Benny?" Melissa had made a

point of excusing herself from a conversation with Les Hylton to check on her young brother.

"Certainly, Melissa. This will be a splendiferous place in which to summer, won't it?"

Melissa sighed with relief and turned back to the others. She must try to control her maternal oversolicitude toward Benny; he was a big boy now and quite capable of taking care of himself.

The task of watching the food had been assigned to Jim Wilson, who hailed from Cape Cod and was an old hand at New England clambakes. Now he sang out, "Clambake's ready. Come and get it!"

No one needed urging; everyone grabbed a plate and made for the steaming and succulent seafood and potatoes heaped high on the sturdy table. Bowls of melted butter for the fish, and sour cream and chives for the potatoes, completed the Lucullan repast. Melissa sat down on a large flat boulder and started attacking the food as though it were her first meal in many days. The savory food plus the flickering lights and fresh salty sea air had made her ravenous. Bob Converse came to join her, his plate already high with empty shells.

"So nice of your family to do this," he said, scraping a space of sand level to use as a makeshift table. "Too bad tomorrow's a workday."

Melissa saw her opportunity and eagerly seized it. "Tell me about your job. Dad mentioned you'd be here for the whole summer."

"Well, I don't know about that. We expect to be, but these assignments are unpredictable. Last month we were on a job that we thought would keep us busy for half a year, and vroom, we found we couldn't go any farther, and that was the end of it."

"I'm intrigued." Melissa batted her eyelashes flirtatiously. "Exactly what is it you do?"

Bob Converse took another healthy swallow of his beer. "Oh, we make underwater explorations for various pur poses. It's a whole other world down there—really fascinating. I've been diving professionally for twenty years and I still find it exciting every time I go down."

"But I don't quite understand. You don't just pick out a spot at random and dive down hoping you'll hit something, do you?" She was aware that the question sounded stupid, but it was asked with a purpose.

"Oh, God, no." He sucked the last bit of juice from a clamshell and added it to the pyramid-shaped mound on his plate. "You see, what we do is rather special. We go down to—well, in this case, for example—"

At that moment a tall shadow appeared and a gruff voice issued a terse command: "Bob, get on with your food before it gets cold. I'm sure Miss Starbuck isn't interested in technical details."

Rod Wilshire towered above them. In the wavering, changeable light Melissa could not see much of the expression on his face, only a muscle that twitched in his jaw. However, she could tell from the tone of his voice that for some reason he was quite perturbed.

She had not expected to have to cope with Rod Wilshire this evening, and he had kept her from finding out more about what Oceanic Surveying was up to. She resented his appearance on both counts. But she did not know why the fluttering in her heart should be so violent.

"I—where did you—? I didn't know—why didn't you—?" She found herself stuttering in confusion.

Was his smile as derisive as she thought, or were the shifting lights merely playing tricks?

"I'll be happy to answer your question, Melissa, as soon as you are able to ask one."

His amused condescension was too much. She cast about for a suitably cutting retort and found one: "Never mind, Mr. Wilshire. I don't believe there's any information I really require from you at the moment. In fact, Bob and I were just going to take a walk along the beach to

60

look for more firewood." She took Bob Converse's arm possessively.

Rod stepped easily in front of them, effectively blocking their way between the large boulder and the table. "Oh?" he asked. "Are you sure your wife won't mind your taking an evening stroll along the beach with a female as deliciously tempting as Miss Starbuck?"

A weighty silence followed. Melissa was nonplussed at Rod's heavy-handed lack of subtlety in reminding Bob Converse that he was a married man, and furious at the implication of his remark. But Rod stood his ground, as implacable as the boulder at his side.

After some moments Melissa recovered her composure and gave a false, tinkling laugh. "Excuse me. I'd better see if anyone wants seconds on the potatoes."

She strode angrily away and only with an effort reverted to the role of gracious hostess. She noticed that Trish Lessing was holding court, with Benny and the Wilsons circled attentively at her feet. Paul and Ellen Starbuck, having seen that all the guests were served, were sitting on a blanket in a dim corner of the party, holding hands like teen-agers. Melissa smiled lovingly as she stopped for a moment to watch them.

A hand suddenly caught her arm from behind, and she turned to find Bob Converse looking at her expectantly.

"Well? How about that walk on the beach?" he said.

She *had* invited him but only in retaliation against Rod Wilshire's extreme rudeness. Now she found she had unwittingly trapped herself. *Well, why not?* She felt suddenly defiant. "Yes, let's go. The fire is getting low. I think I know where some driftwood is, down this way toward the cove."

"Lead on, I'm with you." Bob Converse took her hand, and they wandered out of the circle of light. The moon was high and misty, and they found it necessary to thread their way carefully through occasional patches of rocks and scrub. Bob had been silent from that first sentence, but now he chuckled deeply.

"What are you laughing at?" Melissa, now curious, inquired.

"Trying to figure out what's eating my boss."

"Your boss?"

"Rod. He's the captain of the team. He sure didn't like my talking to you for some reason."

Melissa thought for a minute. "Well, maybe he's just possessed of an incurably nasty disposition. Had you considered that possibility?"

"Nope. That's the funny thing about it: He's usually not like that at all."

"Then your experiences with him must have been vastly different from mine."

In the half-cloudy moonlight he looked at her speculatively. "You serious?" He sounded genuinely surprised, then he chuckled again. "Well, maybe women see him differently. I guess the few who don't love him hate him."

Melissa felt a strange, violent bump against her ribs. "Why? Is he supposed to be a Casanova of some kind?"

Bob Converse countered her question with another. "Wouldn't you say he would be, looking the way he does?"

Melissa tossed her blowing red hair out of her eyes. "I never gave his appearance too much attention." Even to her the words sounded false. She tried to cover their hollow ring with a light attempt at a laugh.

Bob continued, "Although I guess the Bird-woman might be able to keep him under control. She always seems to keep a tight rein on him—"

"The who?"

"Rod's girl. I can never recall her name, but it's something to do with a bird."

Melissa's mind flashed back to the telephone call Rod had received from New York and to the message she had taken. "This lady's name wouldn't be Nightingale by any chance, would it?"

Bob snapped his fingers in recall. "Sure. That's it. Nightingale. Wonder why that's so hard for me to remember?"

"I think we have about enough wood now, don't you?" She had gathered only three or four small pieces, but she realized she was quite chilly. She wanted only to get back to the warmth of the fire and the company of the others.

"Wait a minute, Melissa." He pulled out a crushed pack of cigarettes from the pocket of his jacket and offered her one. When she shook her head, he lighted his own, flicking a windproof lighter into the wind with the practiced hand of a seagoing man. His beard was lightly grizzled with gray, his skin leathery from exposure to wind and sun.

He replaced the cigarettes, tapping them far down into the deep pocket. "I want to clear something up. Rod made a big thing about my being married. I just want you to know my wife and I haven't lived together for several months now. I don't want you to think I'm making a play for you when I don't have any right to." He moved closer to her, tossing his cigarette into the damp sand. He put an arm around her waist and pulled her to him. A strong smell of tobacco and beer emanated from him.

"Wait, Bob," she said, trying in vain to move his arm away, "we're just taking a walk to collect firewood. I mean, this wasn't intended to be a big romantic interlude or anything like that."

He laughed and pulled her closer. "Don't kid me, kid. When I saw those green eyes and that red hair, I had your number. I'm not a bad guy. You'll find out . . ."

Although he was only a few inches taller than she, he was amazingly strong. She tried to push him away with both hands against his chest, but it was like trying to repel a mass of steel.

He gripped her wrists in both hands. "You like to play rough, is that it?"

63

She could feel his heavy breath on her cheek. With all her force, she freed one hand from his grasp and slapped him across the face. The blow was not hard, but it caught him by surprise and he released her other hand, his own moving reflexively to the side of the jaw that had received her slap. She started running wildly back toward the distant lights of the beach party. She could make out the general contours of the shoreline, but the half-buried rocks and flotsam that dotted this deserted area were indiscernible, and her bare strippy sandals offered minimum protection against them. She could dimly hear Bob's voice behind her calling out to her to wait. Unheeding, she began running closer to the line of gnarled shrubbery that marked the beginning of the cliffside. The light was even more limited here, but what was of primary importance was to get back to the others before Bob Converse could overtake her. She was not afraid of his harming her physically; she simply did not want to feel his touch again. The sensation of his arm around her waist had been extremely distasteful.

She sprinted headlong toward the wispy strings of light. All at once she pitched forward; her sandal had caught in a tangle of vine whose tendrils curled stubbornly around her ankle. The sand cushioned her fall; she knew at once she was not hurt. She sat up from her prone position and tried to unsnarl the clinging branches.

"Damn it to hell," she muttered in exasperation. Just as she got the vine loose and began to get to her feet, she felt a firm supporting hand under her elbow.

"I told you not to swear in public, you redheaded wench," Rod Wilshire admonished her in a choking voice. He seemed to be having trouble avoiding laughing at her openly.

Chapter 7

"Get out of my way, please."

She was not in the mood for feeble attempts at humor. She had had quite enough of men—any man, all men—for one evening. But Rod held her arm like a vise, and she was forced to stand still, more or less at his mercy.

She cunningly decided to change her tactics. "Look, Rod, I know your brute strength exceeds mine. You could keep me here all night if you wanted to. But I'm appealing to your innate decency—if you have any. Let me go."

The dig, which had slipped from her mouth unawares, apparently found its mark. He released his hold and stood looking at her irresolutely. Then they both heard the same sound at the same instant: footsteps drawing closer. Rod clapped a hand loosely over her mouth. They heard Bob Converse call her name once or twice, his voice almost lost on the wind. Then his scuffing footsteps went past them, the sound slowly fading.

She exhaled a deep breath. She tried to speak, found she could not, then cleared her throat and tried again. "Let's go back." Her voice was strangely husky; she sounded quite unlike her usual self.

His answer was unequivocal: "No. I want to talk to you." He put an arm about her waist to restrain her, and she felt the same ridiculous helplessness that had overpowered her on the porch when he had first taken her in his arms. But this time she was determined to fight the feeling with every ounce of strength she possessed.

"I don't think we have anything to talk about," she said.

"And I think we do."

His grip tightened. The bones in her body seemed to be slowly dissolving. She hoped she would not disgrace herself by fainting into the sand.

With an effort she managed to make her voice disinterested, toneless: "Then talk, if you think you have anything to say."

"All right. You don't sound as though you'd be the most receptive audience in the world, but. . . . The other night, I know I must have puzzled you by what I did, or didn't do—"

"The other night—when? I don't know what you're referring to."

"Oh, come on, Melissa, don't be a child." His voice snapped with authority. "I haven't forgotten it, and I'm damn sure you haven't either. I mean the way I left you on the stairs."

"Oh." She was pleased that her tone carried just the airiness she was aiming for. "That! Why, I hadn't given that a second thought—"

"I'm going to gag you, damn it, if you don't let me finish!"

She sank into silence. *Let him talk,* she thought balefully. *He'll probably hang himself.*

"I walked away from you, though God knows it was the last thing in the world I wanted to do, because there was some unfinished business I had to take care of in New York—"

"I'm sure there must be loads of unfinished business you have to take care of all over the place."

Even in the murky light she could see the flash of anger in his eyes. "I swear I'm going to do you bodily harm if you don't shut up and listen. Yes, this unfinished bit of business did have to do with a lady, if that's what you're hinting at so smirkingly."

66

"Would that lady be the well-known Bird-woman?" she asked more smirkingly than ever.

"The 'Bird-woman'? Who called her that?" His tone was an odd blend of amusement and anger.

"Your friend and co-worker, Mr. Converse. The man whose clutches I just escaped."

"Oh, Bob. He would come up with something like that. By the way, he's harmless. Slightly pushy on occasion but harmless. But anyway, yes, Tracy Nightingale is the woman in question. She and I have been—had been—'keeping company' I believe is the phrase. For maybe six months. I knew before I went to Greece that she and I were both ready to call it quits. Then when I came back to New York for those two days—the night you cooked me the bacon and eggs—I had made a date to meet her and break it off officially, but she never showed up. She called the next day with a lame excuse about how she'd had to work late and hadn't been able to phone—"

"You know, Rod"—Melissa tried to convey an impression of disinterested superiority—"you needn't feel you owe me any explanation—"

"I'm pretending you didn't interrupt, Melissa." His tone was that of a stern schoolmaster. "At any rate, that's why I left you on the stairs. I didn't want to make any overtures until I could consider myself morally free." She started to speak, but he stopped her with a quick gesture of his upraised hand. "Maybe that sounds ridiculously old-fashioned, but I didn't want to start something with you while there was any entanglement with anyone else. Because, Melis— For God's sake keep your mouth shut for a minute. I knew from the day you almost ran me down on that bicycle—I told you to keep your mouth shut—that you were going to be very important to me. That's why I tracked you down like a bloodhound. You may think I go to such ridiculous lengths every day of my life, but I assure you I've never done a thing like that before and I doubt that I ever will again."

He let out a long breath, as though the effort of the protracted speech had left him spent. Melissa found she had hardly been breathing at all, and she too exhaled deeply. His whole story had left her dumbfounded. She thought he had walked away from her out of lack of interest. Now he was telling her he felt so deeply for her he hadn't wanted to make advances until he was free to give her his undivided— She would not let herself finish the thought. There would be plenty of time later to attach labels to their emotions.

"But—what attracted you to me?" she asked almost shyly.

"I don't know." He thought for a minute. "I suppose it was your ability to convey such strong righteous indignation when you were so obviously in the wrong."

She laughed delightedly, then slowly lifted her arms and put them around his shoulders. She could feel the sharp razor-cut hairs on the back of his neck. A thrill went through her body, and for the first time she offered herself to it fully. She could feel his arms tighten around her fiercely and possessively, his face in her hair.

"My God," he whispered. "This is like nothing else I've ever—" His voice stopped as his lips avidly sought and found hers.

The kiss was at first circumspect, tender. Then, their bodies arched by mutual desire, his mouth opened hungrily and his tongue became a searching invader, her own answering, welcoming the intrusion. On her television show Melissa portrayed a young woman who was madly in love, but she now realized that she had never even imagined this rapturous and all-encompassing feeling of near bliss. Lightly his hand sought the fullness of her breasts, and her excitement increased. His touch was so gentle, yet even his lightest caress hinted at great underlying strength. If at that moment he had ordered her to swim to China or perform some equally impossible feat, she would have tried without hesitation and with all her heart. She had no will of her own, nor did she want to have.

Perhaps he sensed her intense arousal; at any rate, he gently broke off the kiss and looked at her in the hazy moonlight. "You feel as I do, don't you, Melissa?"

It was the first time she could remember that he had ever used her name in just that way. It had usually been a joking nickname: the "tiny mite" or "redheaded wench" or a sarcastically spat "Miss Starbuck." At last he spoke her own name simply and with longing, and it had never sounded so musical to her ears.

She nuzzled the top of her head against his chin and again realized with a shock the disparity in their heights.

"How tall are you?" she asked, awestruck.

"A shade over six feet. How small are you?" In other circumstances the question would have irritated her enormously, but tonight it sounded like an eloquent love poem.

"A shade over five three."

"Well, we know who's boss already, don't we?" He laughed, and she joined his laughter.

"I'm a liberated woman, I'll have you know," she said gaily. "And don't you ever forget it." She sobered suddenly as a thought occurred to her. "By the way, what are you doing here, anyway? I thought you were going to be away for the whole weekend."

"I heard you were having a clambake, so I hurried back to join the festivities." His face, too, grew serious. "No, I went back to New York to straighten matters out with Tracy once and for all. It was easier than I expected, so here I am." He kissed her again, and again what began as a gentle coming together evolved into a passionate melding of their lips and bodies.

"Oh, Rod," she whispered as she held him to her, "I can't believe life can be this perfect, can you?"

"It isn't very often." He moved his hand slowly, lightly, up and down her back, as if to assure himself she was real. "I want never to let you go," he said softly into her ear.

He kissed her again, and she had once more the sensation of throbbing weakness, of drowning, and strangely, at the same time, a feeling of being completely protected by his towering strength. Desire quickened in her like an exquisite pain. She suddenly realized what the expression *to ache for someone* meant. They broke away slightly and looked at each other for a moment in silent wonder. And then their bodies melded again with ever greater urgency. From far away the sound of the eternal waves rose and fell, their languid rhythm a counterpoint to the wildly accelerating beat of Melissa's heart.

The voice, high and distant, was borne down-beach by the wind. When at last it registered in her conscious mind, she realized she had been hearing it for some time. It sounded like Benny, but she could not imagine why he would be searching for her. She moved her face away from Rod's and looked at him uncertainly. She was still not sure whether the sound was real or a trick of wind and surf.

"Did you hear that?"

"Yes," he said quietly. "Someone's calling you. We'd better go. Something must have happened."

When the call came yet again, she heard the urgency that Rod had recognized at once.

"It sounds like Benny," she whispered uneasily.

He took her hand, and they raced together down the beach. The heel of one of her sandals loosened; she did not stop to adjust it but continued her headlong pace, ignoring the stab of pain when she inadvertently struck one of the rugged shore pebbles.

As they drew near the party, she could see a circle of people standing around a prone figure near the fire. Benny ran to meet her. "It's Dad, Melissa."

"Oh, my God," she breathed, and ran toward the motionless body. She knelt beside him only long enough to see the peculiar gray of his face, then looked up accusingly at the circle of figures. "Why doesn't somebody do something?" she cried in a choked voice.

Amelia Harding hurried to her and put an arm around her shoulders. "They've called an ambulance, Melissa. They say he shouldn't be moved till it gets here."

Rod Wilshire elbowed his way through the awed, helpless spectators. "Let me have a look," he said, and something steellike in his inflection melted the watchers out of the way.

He examined Paul Starbuck quickly, taking his pulse with economical efficiency. "We can't wait for an ambulance," he said, then straddled the unconscious man and put his mouth against the colorless lips. He began the deep-breathing process of mouth-to-mouth resuscitation, continuing tirelessly for what seemed to Melissa hours.

His efforts were unflagging until the two white-jacketed men, led by Ellen Starbuck, made their way down the beach steps with a stretcher, lifted Paul onto it, and began the painstaking ascent up the slope to the waiting ambulance. Melissa followed. She tried to crawl into the back of the ambulance behind her mother, but one of the attendants gently stopped her.

"He shouldn't have more than one person in the back with him, miss."

Melissa turned away blindly and was met by Rod Wilshire's waiting arms. "I'll drive you in, Melissa." He led her wordlessly to his car.

On the way to the hospital Melissa sat dry-eyed and composed. Rod, glancing at her with concern as he skillfully maneuvered the car, realized she was in a state of semishock.

Melissa, staring unseeingly at the road ahead, heard a painfully ironic echo of the words she had spoken only a little while before: *I can't believe life can be this perfect, can you?* And Rod's thoughtful, all too prophetic reply: *It isn't very often.*

71

Chapter 8

Two weeks later, on a Saturday misty with warm rain, Paul Starbuck came back to Highcliffe Inn. The heart attack had been serious but not massive. Rod Wilshire had faithfully driven Melissa in to the hospital each afternoon. He would chat with Paul for ten minutes or so, then leave father and daughter alone and pick up Melissa again an hour later.

One day Rod brought Paul Starbuck a model sailboat to help him while away the long hospital hours. When Rod left the room, Paul Starbuck looked over his half-glasses at his daughter. "Good man," he said with New England brevity.

Melissa arched her eyebrows quizzically. "I thought you highly resented him, Daddy," she countered, reverting to her childhood name for her father. "I mean—hadn't you decided that he was going to ruin Nantucket?"

Her father rubbed his chin thoughtfully. "That remains to be seen. I'll reserve judgment on that point. But when a man has saved your life, you're inclined to feel charitable about his flaws."

"Did he literally save your life?"

"So the doctor told me yesterday. He said, without the mouth-to-mouth resuscitation he doubted I'd be around to give him such a hard time."

It was true that Paul Starbuck was far from the ideal patient. In fact, the staff had affectionately dubbed him the "*im*patient." He had wanted to go back to Highcliffe Inn before the first week was out; it took the combined efforts of his family and the hospital staff to convince him to stay.

One day, as they got into Rod's car after a visit during which Paul had been particularly obstreperous, Melissa said impatiently, "I do wish he'd behave himself. I adore my father, but sometimes he can be downright ornery."

Rod drove out of the parking lot offering no reply. Melissa thought for a moment, then said, "But I suppose everyone's parents become problems at times. Were yours?"

He gave her an enigmatic glance as he braked the car for a traffic light. "No, my parents were never a problem to me. They were both killed in a plane crash when I was three."

Melissa felt a sudden urge to slash both wrists. "Oh, Rod. I'm so sorry."

He patted her hand. "It's all right, darling. It was a long, long time ago. And I was lucky enough to be brought up by two very wonderful people." He immediately changed the subject and began telling her an amusing anecdote that had nothing whatever to do with his child-hood.

On their trips to and from the hospital Rod and Melissa held hands and stole a few hurried kisses. But Rod could see that she was understandably preoccupied with her father's illness, and he made no real effort to intrude on her privacy with attempts at serious lovemaking.

After the third or fourth time he had driven her in, Melissa began to worry that Rod was neglecting his own job. "How can you get away from your work like this, Rod?" she asked one day as he cut the car's ignition in the hospital parking lot.

He said nothing for a time, then spoke, seeming to choose his words carefully: "We're at a stage of the job right now where Les Hylton is the expert. He does the preliminary work of—" He stopped short. "I'm just not needed at this particular time, except for an hour or so

74

each day." He grabbed her hand and squeezed it lightly. "Let's go. Your father will be accusing me of kidnapping you."

When Paul Starbuck was at last pronounced fit to be released, the final edict of the doctor was that he must spend less time in the kitchen and more time at recreation. This, to Melissa, seemed a peculiar prescription.

"But, Doctor," she remonstrated, "his favorite recreation is sailing. That's much more strenuous than the work he's been doing in the kitchen."

"But there isn't the same sort of pressure involved, Miss Starbuck. He was advised to leave the advertising business because of having to meet deadlines. Preparing three meals a day for a group of guests has deadlines that are just as inevitable. I'm sure he enjoyed it, but the pressure was there whether he realized it or not."

So it evolved that while Ellen Starbuck was kept busy overseeing the housekeeping end of the operation, Melissa found herself in charge of all the menu planning and a good bit of the actual food preparation. She realized in very short order that Sally Emerson deserved the highest praise; Sally was cheerful, well organized, and calm in the face of any kitchen crisis.

Melissa could not hope to match her father's intricate cuisine, perfected after years of experiment and practice, so she began to plan meals around locally grown produce, with the emphasis on simplicity and freshness. She was usually waiting when the vegetable stalls opened, and took great care in selecting the sweetest corn, the tenderest green beans or squash, the ripest, most luscious tomatoes. After a few days of amusedly watching her make her serious, painstaking choices, several of the farmers began to have baskets of their top-quality produce waiting for her critical inspection.

It was not until her father was back home and obviously improving with every day that Melissa and Rod could have any real time together again. One Saturday morning he came downstairs to find her standing on the porch, a wistful look in her green eyes as she gazed out over the water.

"You don't look like the spitfire I'm used to, Melissa," he remarked softly.

"No." She smiled at him wanly. "Today I feel like a spitfire who's all fizzled out."

It struck him that for the last three weeks she had been subjected to an inordinate amount of strain. Both the worry over her father and the added responsibility of the kitchen had taken their toll.

"What's for lunch today?" he asked.

Puzzled by the seemingly irrelevant question, she thought for a moment and then said, "Vichyssoise and chicken salad. Why on earth do you ask?"

"That's all prepared ahead of time, isn't it?"

"Yes. The soup, of course, will be served cold and the chicken salad was made this morning. Why do you ask?"

"Run upstairs and grab a bathing suit," he ordered briskly. "We're going to have a day to ourselves."

"Rod"—she laughed—"I can't just run off and—"

"Yes, you can," he said firmly. "You've been telling me what a jewel Sally Emerson is. Stop off in the kitchen and tell her you're having the afternoon off. And while you're at it, pick up a big pot, at least two- or three-gallon-sized. An old beat-up one." He patted her lightly on the derrière. "I mean it. Go."

Fifteen minutes later they were driving down the hill, away from Highcliffe Inn.

"This is insane, Rod. Where are we going?"

"You'll see."

He stopped at a fish market and then ducked into the grocery next door, returning to the car with a huge brown bag.

"By the way"—he leaned over and kissed the tip of her nose before starting the car—"I haven't had time to tell you how adorable you look today."

76

When she had gone upstairs for her swimsuit, Melissa had changed into a pair of brief white shorts, a white T-shirt, and a green-shaded white cap.

"Yes," he elaborated, "very nautical."

"Well, that's deceptive," she said. "My experience with sailing is practically nonexistent."

He turned the car away from town and onto Atlantic Avenue.

"How did that happen, since your father is such a rabid sailor?"

"When I was very young, he was working too hard to have much time for it. Then, when he did begin to take more time off from business, I was away at school. Then I started working too hard myself to have much free time."

He nodded but said nothing more. They drove for a little time in the silent peace that happens when two people feel completely at ease with each other. He turned right on Surfside Road, a section of the island Melissa had never seen before. Soon they arrived at the town of Surfside, a village of only a few houses and a shop or two. He drove through the little town, down a narrow lane, over a small rise, and there, spread suddenly before them, was an empty stretch of beach and the glistening Atlantic.

An eastern breeze ruffled the water and diffused the sun's reflection into a trillion diamonds. Melissa wriggled into her black bikini in the car while Rod, who had underdressed in his swim trunks, waited at the ocean's edge.

When he heard her running footsteps on the sand, he turned and drew in his breath sharply. Her petite figure was flawlessly proportioned, the hips curving but slender, her waist tiny, her breasts pertly upturned. As she reached him he caught her jubilantly in his arms and made as if to toss her high into the air and out into the ocean. She screamed in mock panic, and they fell laughing onto the sand.

"Last one in," he yelled suddenly, and dove headlong

into a cresting wave. She watched as he came to the surface spluttering noisily. "Holy cow," he exclaimed.

"Is it cold?" she called out.

"No! No, it's great. Practically lukewarm, really. Wait a minute. Don't come in yet. I've thought of something better." He hurried back and scooped her into his arms. "It's much easier if you hit it all at once."

He waded into the sea for a few yards until the water submerged him to his thighs. She was still bone-dry in his arms.

She looked up at him laughing. "I don't know whether this is such a good—" Her voice was lost in the splash as her body hit the water. Its iciness shocked her into a state of vengeful fury. She started after Rod, but he was swimming rapidly away from her, looking back at her periodically, convulsed at her gyrations.

Once their bodies were accustomed to the biting temperature, however, they found the water delightfully bracing. The foaming, lusty waves that rushed to shore made those of the sound at Highcliffe seem infantile by comparison.

At last Melissa, exhausted by laughter and exertion, spread a beach towel and sprawled onto it while Rod had a final dip. As he walked back to her over the rolling dunes, she roused from a delicious half snooze and watched him approach. His legs were brown and incredibly straight and long; his chest glistened with droplets of water. His hair formed ringlets about his face. He pushed it back impatiently as he walked. His abbreviated blue trunks fit like a second skin and attested to his virility. He sank down beside her and began toweling himself dry.

"How did you know about this place?" she inquired drowsily.

"I—just—I was doing a bit of idle exploring one day." His answer seemed strangely incomplete. "It's pleasant, isn't it?"

"Pleasant?" she protested. "What a pale word! It's fantastic!"

"Hungry?"

"Never hungrier. Can't wait to find out what's in that mysterious brown bag you smuggled into the backseat."

"All in good time, my pet."

They gathered driftwood and soon had a roaring fire going. He fashioned a spit of sorts from three of the sturdier branches, filled the big pot with seawater, then suspended it on the spit. When the water had reached a rolling boil, he took two large wicked-eyed lobsters from the bag and plopped them into the pot. Almost immediately they turned the familiar scarlet associated with the delicious crustacean. Rod brought out a long loaf of crusty bread, a mold of sweet butter, and two lemons. In twenty minutes the lobsters were ready.

Melissa never forgot that meal. The lobster meat was moist and tender, cooked to perfection. Dunking pieces in the melted butter and lemon juice, then tearing off a chunk of the sun-warmed bread, she felt like a true gourmand. Her pleasure was heightened by the background—the dunes around them, the embers of the cooking fire, the inverted bowl of blue sky dotted with scudding, shifting clouds.

Half an hour later, their chins sticky with butter, they braved the biting water again for a wash-up, then collapsed on their towels. Melissa lay breathing long deep breaths, listening to the lazy, sighing wind in the scrub pines and Scotch broom. When she opened her eyes, through her wet curling lashes she could see the scalloped shoreline. The rest of the world seemed to be held at an infinite distance. Part of a poem she had happened on in one of her Nantucket books floated through her mind, and she mouthed the words softly:

"Did you ever hear of 'Sconset where there's nothing much but moors,

And beach and sea and silence and eternal out-of-doors
. . ."

"That's lovely. Did you write it?" There was a low throb in Rod's voice.

"No. A Nantucket poet named Bliss Carmen wrote it. Isn't that a perfect name for a poet?"

"Sea and silence," he mused. "That's what I love about going underwater. A silent, mysterious universe, undreamed of by people who've never explored it. In a way it's as alien to normal life as walking on the moon. Absolute solitude and yet, of course, teeming with life. I think it's the last frontier—on this planet, at least. And an endlessly fascinating one."

Melissa was moved. His voice was lyrical, almost reverent. It was impossible to believe he would do anything to destroy surroundings he loved so much.

Her thoughts were shattered when he rolled over to her quite suddenly and nestled against her body. Instantly a surge of passionate longing permeated her being. She raised her arms to clasp him to her, and his lips came down upon hers, devouring her mouth. Against her side she could feel the tangible evidence of his desire.

"Melissa, do you realize this is the first time we've really been together since the night your father—since the night of the clambake?"

"Of course I do, you idiot," she answered, saying the last word caressingly.

"I want you so much."

"I know."

"I want to make love to you."

She averted her face slightly, and her eyes clouded. She thought he loved her, but he had not actually spoken the words. She knew she loved him, but was she letting herself in for another rejection? Rod Wilshire was the most physically beautiful man she had ever seen. She knew, from what Bob Converse had said, that countless other women

80

agreed with her. Perhaps Rod had so many women standing in line that seducing them thoughtlessly had become nothing more than a pleasurable hobby to him.

His hand began gently to trace the outline of her bikini bra, and all the caution and uncertainty was swept away in a blinding surge of overpowering longing. She turned back to him and let her eyes drink in every part of the face above her: the dampened black ringlets of his hair, the strong dark brows, the almost hypnotic eyes, the full, slightly parted lips. She was unable to resist him. Every physical instinct of her body cried out to have him possess her.

She was about to whisper her surrender when her words were halted by a spattering of huge raindrops. Startled, she looked up and found the sky had darkened with one of the island's summer storms that periodically materialized from the fickle, changing ocean. Angry clouds moved across the face of the sun; the rain swiftly became a downpour.

They began to race about, gathering towels and bags of garbage, throwing them helter-skelter into the car's backseat. They slammed the doors against the sheet of blowing rain and collapsed with helpless laughter.

They could not drive away; visibility was zero. The enormous drops pounded the windshield and roof in a violent tattoo. They sat for a moment, looking at each other and grinning, sharing in conspiratorial silence the snugness of their motorized haven.

"Hell of a time for a rainstorm," Rod observed wryly.

Melissa gave him a faint smile and a nod but said nothing; she was trying to sort out her feelings. Had the downpour been deliverance or intrusion? She could not decide.

Rod slid closer to her on the seat, and her heart lurched. He put a finger under her chin and lifted her face. "You know something?" he asked with a devilish grin. "We're both all wet."

He reached behind him and got a dry towel from the

81

backseat, leaving her to ponder the implications of his remark. Had he meant it only casually and literally, or was he trying to tell her something more serious? The instant the thought crossed her mind she told herself impatiently she was being a goose. Was she turning into the kind of pseudo-psychological ninny who tried to analyze even a simple hello?

Rod began to rub the rough towel across her shoulders, slowly and sensuously. As the damp chill disappeared from her wet body, a deep warmth pervaded her. She felt as though she had just downed a double shot of brandy. He moved a corner of the towel across her eyebrows and wiped the clinging droplets away from her hairline. Every touch of the terry cloth was a caress. He moved the towel to her legs, drying them from thigh to ankle with long smooth strokes.

"Pretty nice pair of legs," he murmured, then gave her a brief grin and resumed his task.

As he bent in front of her, she hesitantly reached out to let her fingers find their way through his dampened mat of dark hair. It felt springy, almost alive in her fingers. She realized she had wanted to do just this since the first time she had seen him. An unsettling thought jarred her reverie. How many other women had looked at that dark, curling mop and felt the same impulse? Perhaps she was the worst kind of trite and unimaginative fool in succumbing to it.

Rod, with that air of abrupt decision she had come to recognize as characteristic, suddenly straightened and wiped a palm across the steamy windshield. "Rain's stopped," he announced, and threw the dampened towel carelessly into the backseat. His face became darkly serious. "Well, I'm tired of fooling around."

Melissa sat waiting, breath suspended. Was he about to tell her quite brutally that she bored him—that their brief flirtation was over? But he was continuing. "I suppose there's only one way to end all this."

Melissa was sure that his next statement would be a plainspoken rejection. He would announce that he was in love with someone else, or that his job was finished and he was leaving Nantucket. She looked out the window, seeing nothing. She began to prepare herself mentally for the blow. Then he caught her cheeks in both hands, turned her to face him, and she saw a ghost of the crooked grin.

"If you're willing," he said softly, "I think we ought to get married."

Chapter 9

The next two weeks passed for Melissa in a delirious blur of happiness. She and Rod had decided to have an autumn wedding in New York, which was, after all, home for both of them.

Ellen Starbuck had greeted the news with unalloyed delight. Since Rod's quick-thinking skill had saved Paul's life on the night of the clambake, she had lavished on him the kind of affection heretofore reserved for her family. She made sure Rod was always furnished with an extra supply of fluffy king-sized towels, and she often left a bouquet of wild flowers on his night table.

Paul Starbuck, too, had accepted the news of the engagement with equanimity, even pleasure. Although he still had reservations about Rod's mysterious salvaging work, he held them in abeyance, for he could not remain immune to his daughter's joy.

Benny alone seemed impervious to the Wilshire charm. He had greeted the news of Melissa's engagement with a blend of resignation and disappointment. One night after dinner Melissa found him reading alone in the Big Room. Puzzled and hurt by his manner, she was determined to find out the reason for it.

"Come on, Benny, 'fess up," she started without preamble. "What's the matter with you? Don't you like Rod?"

Benny closed his book reluctantly, keeping his finger in it as a not-too-subtle hint that he hoped to return to it soon. "Certainly. I consider Mr. Wilshire to be a paragon of virtue and God's gift to women."

Melissa's eyes widened. "I detect an unmistakable note of sarcasm."

"Not at all. *Au contraire.* You should consider yourself honored that you're his chosen mate when practically all the women on Nantucket Island are groveling at his feet."

Melissa's heart gave a startled lurch, but she forced lightness into her voice. "Like who? Or should it be like whom? Anyway, who'd you have in mind?"

"Trish Lessing for instance. And of course the lovely librarian."

Melissa sank to the arm of the sofa, bewildered. She had never known Benny to lie; but, on the other hand, if these outlandish accusations were true, when was Rod finding the time for his extracurricular courtships? He had been with her almost every evening.

"I think you'd better explain, Benny."

Benny looked away from her and seemed to reconsider his words; at any rate, he gave an embarrassed snuffle and shook his head.

"I mean it," Melissa insisted. "I want you to tell me exactly what you're driving at."

"Well"—he licked his lips nervously—"first of all, forget Trish Lessing. He's had nothing to do with her that I know of—"

"Then why did you mention her at all? There must have been some—"

He flicked her a glance, then averted his eyes again. "Well, I might as well tell you the truth. I called Trish up the day after the clambake and asked her to go out with me. She was practically overcome with laughter and said I should call back when I grew up. Then she said if Rod Wilshire was interested, to have him give her a ring." Benny coughed self-consciously. "It was perhaps erroneous of me to have mentioned her."

"Granted. That's really unfair, Benny. I can understand

that your pride was hurt, but still . . ." Even though she was upset, Melissa's sympathy went out to Benny. She remembered from her own growing-up that rejection from the opposite sex could be devastating to an adolescent. "Oh, Benny, there'll be plenty of girls in your life later on. Believe me—"

"I don't know. It seems to me to be perfectly obvious that the female of the species is looking for biceps rather than brains. Physical prowess seems to far exceed mental acuity on her list of important attributes."

Melissa found it difficult to hide a smile. The high-flown intellectual analysis of the situation was so incongruous coming from the mouth of the stringbean sixteen-year-old.

"Trish Lessing probably doesn't deserve you, Benny. Look at it that way." She touched his forehead with the back of her fingers gently, trying to smooth away the worry lines. Then her heart sank as her mind reverted to the other woman Benny had alluded to. "You mentioned Amelia Harding. What gave you the idea that there was anything between her and Rod?"

"Well, that wasn't much either, I guess."

"No. What? You started this and I want to know."

"Well, I mean, after all, it was prior to your engagement. It was just that I overheard them conversing during the clambake. Rod told her he guessed she was tired of his camping on her doorstep."

Melissa felt as though someone had hit her in the stomach. She had not even been aware that Rod Wilshire had known the attractive blond librarian before the night of the beach party. Now it seemed he had been "camping on her doorstep"? It was quite a revelation. On the other hand, it was, as Benny had said, before she and Rod had become deeply involved. In any case, she firmly resolved to give her fiancé the benefit of the doubt and try to put the disclosure out of her mind. It was too nebulous to make a big deal of, and wasn't trust a large part of love?

She tousled Benny's hair affectionately. "I think you

may have misunderstood, Benny. I'm sure there's nothing to it. And I want you to try to get to know Rod better. You'll discover what a wonderful guy he really is."

Following his doctor's orders, Paul had bought a small sailboat secondhand from a Madaket man who was in the market for a larger one. He christened it the *Ellenissa*, a combination of Ellen and Melissa, and began to take it out for short trips to Madaket Harbor two or three times a week. Most of his sailing was done in the early morning before the waters around the island became too crowded with pleasure craft.

Melissa usually went with him on Sundays, when breakfast was served to the guests at a later hour, and she found the dawn excursions in the aging but well-kept twenty-footer a refreshment to body and soul. As they sailed offshore from Dionis Beach and rounded Eel Point before putting into Madaket Harbor, the faint light fingers of dawn slowly, almost imperceptibly, dispelled the night mists. Usually, as they heeled into the harbor, the rising sun would just be appearing across the water in front of them, like a slowly awakening red giant. The view was spectacular in the true sense of the word, and Melissa began to understand why sailing held such fascination for her father. She also learned to appreciate even more the miraculous spirit of the Nantucket whalers of the eighteenth and nineteenth centuries.

For she quickly discerned that sailing was an occupation that one could never grow complacent about. Even on the calmest days one's wits and skill were constantly kept alert by sudden tides and eddies. To think of those intrepid men, once their whaleboats had been lowered, in a vessel no longer than the one in which she now sat! And they were not only battling the dark uncharted seas but also attempting to overpower a sea mammal often more than five times the length of their frail craft.

One day she was trying to express her admiration and

awe of such men, and it occurred to her that Paul Starbuck might not share her views in light of his strong belief in protecting the delicate balances of nature and the environment. She paused in mid sentence and looked at him questioningly. "I suppose you don't agree that they were such heroes, Dad. In light of today's 'Save the Whales' and 'Save the Seals' and—"

He shook his head at her lack of comprehension. "One thing has almost nothing to do with the other, Lissa. Those men were earning a precarious livelihood in the only way they knew how. The product they were going after—whale oil—was essential for human beings who used it to light their homes. Whales were in no way an endangered species at that time. Do you think there's any way I, who was born and bred in Nantucket with Starbuck for a name, wouldn't share your veneration of those men?"

She nodded, relieved. Then she remembered something else. "Dad, Rod asked me the other day whether we're actually descended from the Mr. Starbuck in *Moby Dick.* I had to admit to him I'd never asked you about it."

Paul Starbuck chuckled. "Well, that's a matter of conjecture. Of course, I suppose every Starbuck in these parts was related to him in some way or other. On the other hand, Melville may simply have seen the name somewhere on the island and chose it because he liked the sound of it. I don't believe it's known whether Mr. Starbuck was an actual living first mate." He looked at Melissa intently. "You've read *Moby Dick,* haven't you, honey?"

"I hadn't till this summer, I'm sorry to say. Then I sat up far too late every night for a week till I finished it."

"Let's see if I can remember that favorite quote of mine—I mean in reference to Nantucket. I believe it goes: 'And thus have these naked Nantucketers, these sea hermits, issuing from their ant-hill in the sea, overrun and conquered the watery world like so many Alexanders.' "

Melissa went home that day feeling deeply blessed that she came of such brave and dauntless stock.

She tried to interest Benny in Nantucket history, for he continued to wander about the hotel trying unsuccessfully to find a useful niche. He had tried to help Jason with carpentry jobs once or twice but obviously found them to be without interest. His only two real pleasures were swimming and stargazing for hours every evening through the telescope he had brought with him from school. And he continued his solitary yoga exercises.

Melissa voiced her concern about Benny to Rod, who soon after found a solution that was at least a temporary improvement. One of the casual friends Rod had made since coming to Nantucket was Chris Petty, who ran a divers' shop in town called The Sunken Vessel. Chris happened to mention to Rod one day that he needed another helper for the summer, and Rod in turn mentioned it to Benny. To Melissa's surprise, Benny applied for the job the next day and got it.

Thereafter, whenever Melissa had an occasion to visit Benny's room, she found it strewn with oceanographic maps and books. He deserted his telescope and began to work very long hours at the shop. Melissa regretted that she now saw him only infrequently, but was glad he had found an interest that absorbed him.

Rod's work, too, had apparently entered a stage where his presence was required at the site for long and irregular periods, and he and Melissa only occasionally managed to steal a few hours together for themselves. Saturday night had become a special time for them; Rod's workweek was ended and Melissa's responsibilities were also lighter, since on Saturday night many of the Highcliffe guests opted for a change of scenery and dined out.

A week or so after the lobster cookout, when that sudden storm had somehow served as the catalyst for Rod's proposal, he burst through the swinging doors into the kitchen where Melissa was busy writing the menu for the following day. To Melissa's amazement, he approached not her but Sally Emerson. Putting an arm casually about the woman's ample waist, he whispered in her ear confidentially. Whatever he said was presumably a question, for Sally turned, gave a conspiratorial smile in Melissa's direction, and nodded.

Rod turned to Melissa. "Melissa, Sally says you're being a terrible nuisance in here, and she longs to get rid of you for a night. So why don't we take her at her word and go out on the town? You and I have both been all-work-and-no-play for quite a while now."

Melissa's eyes shone. She had not taken an entire evening off in weeks, and the idea of going to a restaurant and being only a guest was irresistible.

"You've got a date, Mr. Wilshire. And it would be very dangerous for you to try to renege!"

"I'll make the reservations right away. Meet you in the Big Room at seven."

After a long and languid bubble bath Melissa went through the clothes in her closet trying to decide what to wear. If Rod was taking her to a place that required reservations, she should probably choose something fairly dressy. At last she selected a dress of blue voile. Its lines were simple: a deeply scooped and rounded neck above a wrapped waist and a circular swooping skirt. She added a long strand of tiny opalescent shells she had found in a Nantucket shop and a pair of sandals with the highest heels she had ever dared buy. Taking a last look in the mirror, she decided with pleasure that she looked sophisticated and poised. The thought came to her with a shock: Rod had never seen her really dressed up! All summer she had been in a simple blouse and skirt, or in shorts or jeans.

She had rather dawdled over the finishing touches, and when she walked down the stairs into the Big Room, Rod was already standing before the fireplace. He wore the same cream-colored jacket he had appeared in that first night at dinner, this time with navy trousers. Again she was struck by the classical perfection of his face and form. A moment later he turned and saw her. The care she had taken in dressing was evidently well worth the effort, for his eyes kindled at once with admiration. He held her at arms' length as he surveyed the total result of her toilette.

"Where has my tiny mite gone? And who is this willowy woman of the world sent to replace her?" he asked.

Melissa laughed. "I don't know where that little shrimp went. But I hope I'll be an acceptable substitute."

He took her in his arms. The few guests lingering in the room looked at the couple with either indulgence or envy.

As they neared the center of town he said ruefully, "Oh, I forgot to tell you—I suppose I had underestimated the Saturday night demand for reservations. I tried three places and none of them could take us. But if you'd like to see where we *might* have dined . . ."

They passed the majestic Jared Coffin House, a restored whaling mansion dating from 1845; then Le Languedoc with its impressive garden; and finally, a couple of blocks away, the historic India House, another beautifully restored manor house.

"Well, my spirits refuse to be dampened," she said exuberantly, "though I appreciate the sentiment. Those places look superspecial. But since we can't be really elegant, why don't we go all out for informality?"

"You're the navigator. I'll follow you to the ends of the earth."

A mischievous twinkle sprang into her eyes. She suddenly knew exactly where she would take him. She instructed him to go west and north, and within minutes they were back at Steamboat Wharf. As their location dawned on him slowly, he looked at her and began to laugh.

"Don't you think this is fitting?" she inquired, a devilish gleam in her eyes. "That we return to the scene of the crime?"

Now, both giddy with the spontaneous fun of the mo

ment, they crossed the very spot on South Beach Street where Melissa's bicycle had collided with Rod's duffel bag. Laughingly they went into The Skipper, an animated place crowded with chattering young people. It had an air of easygoing informality about it. They were very lucky to have only a fifteen-minute wait for a table and were seated at one that looked out over the water. The entire restaurant gave its patrons the feeling of being on a boat, for indeed the striped-awning structure had been built from the hull of a ship now moored almost entirely over the water.

"This is fun," he admitted. "But I think you've led me to the most touristy place in town."

"What's wrong with that? To me it's a luxury to be just a tourist for a night!"

He ordered a bottle of white wine to accompany the succulent scallops, clams, and shrimp.

"Not quite up to my father's," she said, "but close." She became serious for a moment. "Rod, how long will this job of yours last? I know Jim and Jerry Wilson went back into New York the other day and—"

He took her hand, and his face became somber. "Melissa, you've got to cure yourself of that awful curiosity about my work. It isn't that interesting. We're way over on the other side of the island. It doesn't interfere with the beach around Highcliffe Inn in any fashion whatsoever, and you must just keep your cute but inquisitive little nose out of it."

She was momentarily taken aback by his bluntness. He had always been somewhat taciturn about his work, but he had never told her to shut up, which in effect was what he was doing now. And where exactly was "the other side of the island"? Had he deliberately kept the location vague?

But such a distant shadow could not cloud her evening, and her former ebullience soon reasserted itself.

While they were lingering over their coffee, he took her

hand and squeezed it lightly. "You've been a very good girl since we became engaged."

She eyed him wonderingly. "Why?"

"You haven't nagged me once about not giving you a ring."

Her mouth opened in astonishment. Not until this moment had it occurred to her that a ring was customary under the circumstances.

Rod laughed at her expression, then reached into the pocket of his jacket. "Maybe this will make up for the oversight." He offhandedly extended a small dark blue velvet box.

The glittering diamond solitaire that lay in the folds of ivory satin was the most beautiful jewel she had ever seen. He took it from her trembling hand and slipped it on the proper finger.

"Oh, Rod." Its beauty, flashing in the amber light, was almost hypnotic. Tears sprang to her eyes, and she made no move to brush them away. After a long moment she said softly, "It even fits perfectly. How did you manage that?"

He winked and grinned. "With a little help from your mother."

"This is truly the happiest day of my life. I know that sounds trite, but I don't know how else to express it."

"I know. The deepest feelings are the hardest to talk about."

As they left the restaurant Melissa found herself considering the remark. How odd it was that it should be so true.

Chapter 10

When Melissa showed the engagement ring to her father the next morning during their early Sunday sail, his eyes misted sentimentally as he observed, in silent wonder, her effervescent happiness; her radiance outshone the brilliance of the ring itself. His last lingering doubts about Rod Wilshire's trustworthiness seemed to vanish like the dawn mists clearing over the gray water. Overhead, seagulls swooped and wheeled against the coral sky, mewing greedily as they dove for leftovers from yesterday's fishing boats. As Paul made the turn into Madaket Harbor he adjusted the sail swiftly and skillfully, high-spiritedly imitating the cries of the circling birds.

Watching him, Melissa mused that the doctor's orders for her father to resume his sailing had indeed worked wonders. Paul was more relaxed than she had seen him in a long time. His former brief displays of temper were now practically nonexistent; he seemed refreshed in both body and spirit. He was gradually making quite a decent sailor out of his daughter, and that, too, seemed to give him a great deal of pleasure.

Melissa was therefore dismayed and bewildered by her father's behavior four days later. She was reading in the family's private sitting room in the mid-morning lull between breakfast and lunch when her father entered from one of his sailing trips. She glanced up quickly to greet him, and her eyes were held by the taut expression on his face. His lips were tight, and he seemed to be controlling himself with difficulty.

She decided to lead into the conversation casually. "Dad, hi, did you have a good sail?"

He stopped and looked at her, apparently weighing a decision of some kind in his mind. Then he shook his head slightly, as if to clear it, and muttered, "I'm hot and tired. I think I'll have a cold shower, honey. Go on with your reading."

It was not until after lunch that she was able to have a real talk with him. Ellen had gone into town to do some shopping, and Melissa and her father again found themselves alone in the sitting room. Her father was ostensibly reading a newspaper, but there was a restlessness about him that Melissa found disturbing. At last she went to his chair, put her arms around his shoulders, and kissed the top of his head.

"Daddy," she said softly, "what happened on the sailing trip this morning?"

He raised a hand and patted hers. "Nothing, honey."

"Something did," she persisted. "You weren't very happy when you returned today."

He sighed and gave her hand a squeeze. "Sit down for a minute, please, Melissa."

She obeyed at once, curling her feet under her in a corner of the chintz-covered sofa opposite him.

He looked at her gravely for a long moment before he spoke. "You were very perceptive to see that I was upset when I came in from sailing. I was trying awfully hard to keep you from knowing anything was amiss."

She was more puzzled than ever. His tone was quiet, but there was something both ominous and sorrowful in it. "But what, Dad? For heaven's sake, what's wrong?"

"It's about Rod."

"Rod?" All her senses were instantly alert. "What's happened to him?"

He tried to calm her consternation with a small wave

of his hand. "Nothing's happened to him. I didn't mean to alarm you. It's something I found out this morning when I was sailing."

"Then please tell me." Her voice was sharper than she intended. But her father seemed to be taking a circuitous route in getting started.

"Yes, all right." He looked at her and smiled oddly. "Rod told you he was working way over somewhere on the other side of the island, right, Melissa?"

"Yes. That's what he said just the other night."

"Well, this morning I felt rather more adventurous than usual on my sailing trip, so I went farther out in the sound than I usually do, off Dionis Beach. I saw a strange contraption in the water ahead, couldn't figure out what it was, and decided to investigate. Rod's crew has got a rig set up about two miles offshore—"

"Wait a minute." Melissa felt as though she had been suddenly plunged into a world of fantasy, and tried to force herself back to reality. "First of all, why do you think it's Rod's crew?"

"Because the equipment is marked 'Oceanic Surveying.' How much more proof does anyone need?"

"But there must be some logical explanation. I can't believe all this. There's got to be a mistake. I mean, it was so recently that he told me they were on the other side of the island off a desolate stretch of beach—"

"I hate to say this, Melissa, and I hope you'll believe that, but it seems pretty obvious to me that Rod lied to you."

"Oh, no, I can't believe—"

Paul Starbuck had been controlling his volatile temper with great difficulty up to this point, Melissa realized later. Now he suddenly found it impossible to keep his seething fury inside. "He's lied to you and to all of us. He's the reckless opportunist and adventurer I thought he was from the beginning. He's out there digging on the ocean bottom, using those gigantic suction machines, ruining the— He's a sea scavenger, looting the ocean for—"

"Daddy, please calm yourself and let's try to sort this out rationally." Melissa was having difficulty keeping her own temper reined in. The words her father had used— "reckless opportunist," "sea scavenger"—reverberated through her brain like an insistent and obscene refrain. Those words did not describe the Rod she had come to know and love—not even remotely. Instead, it was this man opposite who seemed to be suddenly alien to her. However, she took a deep breath, and a cooler part of her mind prevailed. "Please, stop pacing and sit down for a minute, Dad. First of all, why would Rod and his company be interested in that particular area?"

"Have you ever heard the name *Andrea Doria?*" her father asked after a pause.

She shook her head, totally bewildered. "Andrea Doria? No, who is she, a friend of the family or—?"

He smiled briefly. "Well, there's no reason why you should have. She went down shortly after you were born ... 1956, I think. She was an Italian liner that was rammed by another ship in these waters south of Nantucket and sank. Fifty people lost their lives, although the great majority were rescued. But, in any case, there have been several efforts since then to bring her up, but the waters have always proved too treacherous. There have always been all sorts of rumors about priceless stolen jewels smuggled aboard by an Italian nobleman who perished in the shipwreck. I think it's quite possible that Rod and his crew have come up here to see if they can do what no one else has been able to do in all those years: find the treasure aboard the *Andrea Doria.*"

"Then why would he have said 'the other side of the island'?"

"Smokescreen, I guess. They don't want to share the wealth."

How could she refute such an argument when she knew

nothing about the story? She sat silently, twisting her fingers together, hoping that some all-knowing heavenly force would give her the wisdom to find the right words.

At last she said evenly, "I think we should give Rod a chance to tell his side of the story before we jump to conclusions."

"Can you imagine what the beaches around here are going to look like before the end of the summer? I tell you, they're not many miles offshore. Just let the wind turn in the wrong direction or a bad storm blow up, and we'll have so much silt and debris washing up on these beaches that—"

She could feel the heat of the anger that flushed her face as she jumped to her feet. "Just a minute! I'm sorry, but I'm not going to listen to any more! You're hanging Rod without letting him have his day in court—you're the judge and the jury all rolled into one! Can't you be fair enough even to wait for him to come back and defend himself? This is a witch-hunt!" When she heard the shrillness in her voice, she forced the tumbling, bitter words back in her throat and made herself sit down again. *My God*, she thought, *what have I been saying? I can't attack my father like this. I've got to think of his well-being above everything, no matter what he says.*

Her father continued his tirade about plundering the ocean and destroying the beaches. She leaned back against the upholstery of the sofa and closed her eyes as she fought against voicing a sharp retort. The only way she could keep from using anger against anger was to get out of her father's presence and try to untangle her own thoughts. When this realization hit home, she rose and, not looking at Paul Starbuck, ran from the room.

She entered her bedroom in a daze and looked at the bedside clock. It was only a little past three; she would not have to begin her work in the kitchen for another hour. She lay down on the bed hoping she could calm herself with a nap. After five minutes she knew that that goal was unattainable. Although her body was drained from the unhappy and confusing quarrel, her mind darted crazily from one unlikely explanation to another. She felt like a deranged mouse trying to find its way out of a diabolical maze.

She got up and put on a well-worn pair of jeans and a T-shirt. She needed some fresh air to clear her head. She got on her bike and coasted down the lane that led to Cliff Road. In contrast with her muddled thoughts, the day was clear and brilliant. A little hotter than was usual in Nantucket, but still the wind on her face was far preferable to the stagnant air of her bedroom.

It was a busy Thursday afternoon in the center of town. Many tourists managed to squeeze in an extra day on their weekend trips, and Thursday had come to be almost as jammed with off-islanders as the weekend proper. They were wandering the cobblestone streets in groups of twos or threes, asking directions, laughing, browsing, and generally enjoying themselves. They seemed completely carefree at this, the very beginning of their holidays, and with an aching envy Melissa noted their air of *joie de vivre*. The explosive happiness that she had come to take for granted over the last few weeks had suddenly deserted her; the bubble had burst with sickening speed.

After a time her spirits lifted a little, and she gave herself a stiff lecture. There was certainly no reason to be a Gloomy Gus until she saw Rod. She would confront him with the story, and he would have a plausible, satisfying answer. It was as simple as that. Her father would be mollified, and everything would be as it had been. So what was there to worry about?

She forced her mind into a practical turn. As long as she was downtown, she might as well accomplish a few errands. She went first into Mr. Tribble's hardware store to see about some weather stripping for the almost completed dining deck, but the material had not arrived. She stopped at the post office for a roll of stamps. Feeling well pleased with herself, she biked down the street to the Atheneum. There was a new book she wanted to ask about.

The town was so crowded that she could not find an empty bicycle rack in her usual spot and had to proceed for half a block farther. Almost everyone who came to Nantucket without a car made a first stop at one of the bicycle rental shops and so were provided with easy and inexpensive transportation for the holiday.

She went up the wide sweeping steps of the library. The doors were closed, but she knew that often the most effective means of combating the somnolent summer heat was to shut one's doors against it. As she reached the heavy double doors, however, she saw a small card attached to one of the knobs: "Back in ten minutes." Looking for a diversion while she waited, she saw diagonally down the block a small brick-paved lane she had never explored. Nantucket Town was full of such hidden byways—they were one of the island's most delightful serendipities.

She passed through the arch of trees that shaded the lane almost completely, turning it into a deep green summer bower. The houses here were built close to the lane, separated sometimes by only a low wrought-iron fence, more ornamental than functional. One house, however, was set farther back, half hidden from the lane by a high white trellis. Through the fence Melissa could hear a low buzz of conversation, as desultory as the hum of bees in the sleepy afternoon. Then she saw a discreet white sign: "Crown and Coronet. Cocktails."

Intrigued, she peered through the dark green tendrils of vine that curled about the trellis. Six or seven tables were dotted about the courtyard, the trees above serving as leafy natural umbrellas. Only three of the tables were occupied: one by a family of four, one by a larger party who seemed to be students on holiday. Sitting at the third, holding hands and engaged in intimate conversation, were Rod Wilshire and Amelia Harding.

Chapter 11

Melissa turned and blindly ran back out of the lane and into the stark white sunlight. Once she was hit by the heat and bustle of the open street, the image of Rod and Amelia leisurely sipping drinks in the deep green garden seemed almost a hallucination. Had her mind become temporarily unhinged by the contretemps with her father? No, the vision had not been an aberration. The memory of their joined hands, of Amelia's face upturned to Rod as if drinking in his every word, was too concrete to have been a figment of her imagination.

She wheeled her way out of the center of town and took a road that looked as though it would lead away from the noise and the crowds. Within minutes she found herself on a narrow country lane paved just enough to keep her bicycle wheels from miring in the marshy sand. Gently rising over dunes, then descending into a miniature valley, the roadside was bordered by a profusion of summer flowers—Queen Anne's lace, small blue violetlike clusters low to the ground, and pink and yellow day lilies. She realized after a time that she was on the road leading to Swain's Mill.

She parked her bike and sat down at the foot of the mill. The landmark windmill, which was still operable, was veneered in the weather-beaten gray shingles that clothed so many of the island's buildings.

She had to give herself a chance to think. Looking at her watch, she saw that it was almost four, time to start dinner preparations. She tried to remember the menu for that night and recalled with relief that it was nothing that required much advance work; Sally could handle it with no big problem.

In any case, her mind was screaming for silence in which to sort things out. If her world had not been brought down in two almost simultaneous crashes, perhaps her mental processes would not have been floundering so wildly. The Scotch brooms on the dunes were slanted at a forty-five-degree angle by the capricious summer wind, as if caressed by an unseen cosmic hand. She watched them, fascinated by the precision of their shifting dance. Such order in nature, and such enviable peace.

Could her father have been right about Rod from the beginning? If it had been only a matter of the odd location of the diving crew, she would certainly have confronted Rod in the certainty that he could explain it away. But seeing him with Amelia Harding in such an intimate and clandestine setting after the remark Benny had repeated to her—how far could the long arm of coincidence be stretched? She would be a fool to ignore such doubly damning evidence, one instance—far from being hearsay —seen with her own two eyes!

On this serene and lovely midsummer afternoon Melissa Starbuck wished with all her heart that she had never come to Nantucket. She wanted to be back in the safe womb of her New York routine, where tomorrow offered no chore more challenging than learning lines for her television show.

She wondered what would happen if she should call the producer and tell him she was ready to return to New York and rejoin the program earlier than she had anticipated. Of course, they could not write her in immediately; they worked several weeks ahead. But when actors were "written out" for a period of time, it was not unusual for the writers to work around them—that is, to manage a way to proceed with the story without the actor, although he would have been useful if available. Perhaps if they knew she could come back to the city, they could use her profitably.

Yet how could she leave her family? The doctor had told Paul Starbuck to turn over his work responsibilities to someone else, and the someone else had been Melissa. She could not escape back to New York and dump the planning and shopping responsibilities back in her father's lap for the remainder of the summer. On the other hand, Sally Emerson was probably quite capable of doing the menu planning in addition to the rest of her chores. Perhaps Sally's daughter, Doris, could work a few extra hours a week to take a part of the burden off her mother.

Melissa's mind went off on still another tortured tangent. If the argument with her father had been upsetting to her, it must have been twice as damaging to him. She had known since she was little more than a baby that she and Paul shared the same weakness: notably, an inability to control their tempers. Perhaps her staying on in Nantucket, far from being helpful, would be the worst thing she could do. If her interest was in protecting her father's health, maybe that interest would be served best by her returning to New York.

As for Rod Wilshire . . . she remembered again that early incident on the stairs when he had left her so abruptly and without a word of explanation. Perhaps he was just continuing with a more elaborate and convoluted version of the same game. Maybe the conquest of women was a sport to him, like fishing. Lure them till they're hooked; reel them in slowly; and if you weary of them, tear the hook away and toss them back into the pond.

At last she remounted her bicycle and headed for Highcliffe Inn. She realized despairingly that she was no nearer a solution than she had been when she sat down at the mill nearly an hour before. She was incapable of further mental torment, solution or no. At the foot of the hill leading to

Highcliffe she got off the bike and walked it up; she had no strength left in her to ride.

Ellen Starbuck stood on the porch, her arms folded across her chest. As Melissa drew near she saw an odd, steely glint in her mother's eye. "I've been waiting for you, Missy." Ellen said. There was hardly any Virginia drawl at all in her words. On the contrary, her voice was crisp and importunate, and her use of Melissa's childhood name was a sure sign that the conversation was going to be a serious one. "I want to talk to you about your father."

"Where is Dad?" asked Melissa uneasily as Ellen ushered her into the second-floor sitting room.

Ellen, her back toward Melissa as she made for a chair, did not turn to look at her daughter. "He's walking on the moors, I think. When I came back from shopping, he told me about this afternoon's 'discussion' the two of you had."

Melissa started to speak, but her mother overrode her. "Melissa, you must know that your father simply cannot be upset. Not by Rod Wilshire, not by you, not by anyone. He must be kept quiet, and he must live in peaceful surroundings." She looked at Melissa's stricken eyes, and her voice softened. "I know you want that for him as much as I do, darling. It's only that when the two of you get angry at the same time and at each other—well, peace flies out the window. Now, I don't understand what this business with the diving crew is all about—?"

She broke off questioningly as Melissa started to speak. But no defense issued from the girl's mouth. How could she defend Rod in the light of what she had witnessed later in the day?

"Did you want to say something, Melissa?"

Melissa shook her head dumbly. Then her innate sense of fairness forced her to blurt out, "But shouldn't we wait till he's had a chance to explain, Mother?" He should surely be given that courtesy, she thought, no matter what happened between the two of them.

"I agree with you completely, Melissa, and I would be

106

very happy to do that. But that explanation will have to wait. Rod called—oh, not more than half an hour ago— and said he wouldn't be here tonight. He had to make a rush trip into New York."

Melissa, though surprised, did not feel nearly as shocked and miserable as she would have expected. Her beleaguered heart had slipped into a realm of numbness that was immune to any further assault. "I see," she responded.

Her mother gave her a quick sidewise glance. Now that she had reproached her daughter, perhaps less gently than she had intended, it was borne in on her that Melissa had looked somehow lost and bewildered from the time she had arrived back from town. Ellen felt that she herself must have been extraordinarily agitated not to have registered the fact at once.

"He'll be gone for the weekend, Melissa. He asked me to tell you."

A rush trip? It was Thursday afternoon. Perhaps he and Amelia Harding were planning a long weekend in New York. A puzzled frown clouded her face. If he had called half an hour ago, the trip must have been sudden indeed. It was only an hour or so ago that she had seen him with Amelia in that garden lounge. The only explanation she could think of was that Rod and Amelia had been overcome with mutual passion and had arranged a hedonistic spur-of-the-moment weekend together, off the island where they could have complete privacy and would not be observed by waifs peering through fences into private gardens. She realized she was letting her imagination run away with her, but she could not control the tears that began to flow down her cheeks.

Ellen Starbuck looked at her daughter, then came to her and held her close. She did not know the reason for Melissa's tears. She suspected they must have been unleashed by more than her daughter's contrition over the argument with her father. But in Melissa's mind it was forever to her

107

credit that her mother asked no questions. She simply held the unhappy girl close and smoothed her disheveled fiery-red hair.

"Oh, darling," Ellen said in a voice that was little more than a whisper, "whatever's bothering you, I'm so sorry." She began to massage the tenseness out of Melissa's shoulders. "Don't worry about the little upset with your dad. Things blow over with him as quickly as they do with you. By Monday morning, when Rod comes back, I'm sure everyone will be in a much better frame of mind for coping with everything."

Melissa, her head buried in her mother's shoulder, asked in a curious muffled voice, "Is that when he's coming back—Monday morning?"

"I don't really know. I only said Monday because I assume he has to be back at work by then. If he's gone for the weekend, he surely won't be back until Sunday. Why, dear?"

"Nothing. I just wondered."

"Look, Melissa." Ellen Starbuck rose and began to speak energetically as if she had just had a brilliant idea. "Why don't you have a nap in your room? Don't even bother to come down for dinner if you don't feel like it. I can handle the desk, and Doris can help her mother in the kitchen if necessary." She took Melissa's chin in her hand and tipped the girl's face upward. "Wouldn't that be nice—to play a lady of leisure for a change?"

As a matter of fact, thought Melissa gratefully, it sounded like a wondrous salvation—at least for the moment. She would not have to see her father tonight, it would give them both additional cooling-off time, and she would not have to cope with serving dinner, a task that seemed beyond her at the moment. She squeezed her mother's hand gratefully, blew her nose on a tissue Ellen clairvoyantly thrust at her, then went to her room and closed the door.

* * *

108

She thought later that it must have been about nine that night when her mother had rapped lightly on the door and, getting no answer, tiptoed in with a sandwich and a glass of milk which she had placed by Melissa's bed. After Ellen had left the room, Melissa, who had only been feigning sleep, had turned over and looked at the tray through swollen eyes and smiled. Maybe later she could eat something.

During the night she had rolled and tossed, her sleep perturbed by bizarre, surrealistic dreams. In the most vivid of them she and Amelia Harding were in two children's swings in a deep, hidden forest. They both heard heavy steps moving through the underbrush, so loud they sounded as though they were made by a prehistoric animal. But when the creature came into view, it was Rod Wilshire dressed in a sinister black diver's suit with a diver's mask and huge black flippers. He began to push the swing that Melissa sat in. At first she laughed with delight at the free-flying sensation. But then he sent her higher and higher into the air. She tried to tell him he was pushing too hard, that she was frightened, but he only laughed. At last she lost her grasp on the swing and was flung clear, spinning dizzily high over the treetops. She looked back once to see that Rod had begun gently pushing the swing in which Amelia sat.

The next morning Melissa went downstairs early to make coffee. She went into the kitchen, still in her robe, and was nonplussed to find her father already there. Perhaps he, too, had had a restless night.

There was an awkward silence for a moment, then he said, "There's coffee already on if you want some."

"Thank you."

She stood irresolutely, wanting to find the words that would make everything all right between them, but no words came. Sally Emerson came in and even she was unusually silent. After a time Melissa crept back upstairs with her coffee and drank the bitter brew in tearless despair.

When she went back down to help serve breakfast, her mother met her at the foot of the staircase and said with false brightness, "Melissa, why don't you take the desk this morning and I'll take over your kitchen chores. Be a nice change of pace for everyone, don't you think?"

Melissa took her place behind the desk and absently picked up a magazine undoubtedly left there by Doris. She knew why Ellen had insisted on trading places with her for the morning: She wanted to keep peace in the family, and therefore she must have known Paul Starbuck was still angry with his daughter. She really should not stay here if her presence was going to be a continued thorn in her father's side. It would be easier for the Starbucks to confront Rod Wilshire with his transgressions—or imagined transgressions—if they did not have to weigh their words out of consideration for Melissa.

The image on the open page of the magazine sprang out at her. It was a magazine for daytime television fans, and Melissa was suddenly confronted with her own photograph. How carefree and happy she looked! In retrospect, she *had* been carefree and happy at the time. No family misunderstandings, no tearing, unfathomable relationship with an unpredictable man. She stared at the picture enviously, as though the girl in it were someone she had never met. And then she knew what course she should follow.

She went downtown after breakfast and did the produce shopping. She brought the vegetables back and gave them to Sally. The day's menus were posted on the cork bulletin board in the kitchen. Everything seemed under control there. She went to Doris Emerson, now on duty at the desk.

"Doris, I have to make a few telephone calls, and it'll be easier for everyone if I make them from the switchboard. Then I won't have to bother you every time I pick up the phone. Okay?"

"Sure, Lissa. I'll be out on the porch getting some sun. Just yell when you're ready for me to take over again."

"Right. Thank you, Doris."

A quarter to eleven. It would be a good time to catch Mr. Hartstone in his office. Plenty of time for him to have gotten settled and too early for him to be out to lunch. She dialed the New York area code and his private office number. After a few rings his secretary answered.

"Hi, Phoebe. This is Melissa Starbuck. Is Mr.—"

"Melissa! For goodness sake, what are you doing back in town? I thought you were away for the whole—"

"I'm not back in town. I'm calling from Nantucket. Is Mr.—"

"Nantucket! Gee, what a great place to spend the summer. We've been having a heat wave, maybe you've heard. This concrete jungle is driving me right up the wall—"

"I know, Phoebe. It must be awful. Look, is your boss in?"

"Ooops, sorry. Forgot you're on long distance. Just a minute."

Evan Hartstone came on the line within seconds. "Melissa! What a great surprise! How's everything going?"

"Well—fine, Mr. Hartstone. Except I—that is, if you should need me for anything, I could arrange to come back for a week or so."

"Are you kidding? This must be mental telepathy. I just got out of a meeting with the writer and director. There's a dream sequence coming up next week, and we were all trying to figure out how to do it without you. Thought we might have to go back and use one of the old tapes."

Melissa's knees felt weak. She had, she realized, not expected such ready acceptance of her offer. Had her impulsiveness taken her further than she was really prepared to go? Well, it was too late now. She was the one who had volunteered.

"Oh. Well, that's wonderful. When would you need me?"

"Monday morning if you can make it."

"Fine. I'll see you then. Usual time and place?"

"That's right. Terrific, Melissa. Oh, wait a minute—I'll have a messenger leave a script at the desk of your building so you'll have a chance to study it a little. It won't be a heavy day for you."

"Wonderful. Thank you, Mr. Hartstone."

Melissa hung up, then picked up the phone again and dialed Nantucket's Memorial Airport to find out what time she could get a plane. The sooner she could get away from the island, the better off everyone would be—at least for a while.

Chapter 12

There was a plane leaving the island for New York at five forty-five that afternoon. That should be about right; it would give her plenty of time to pack and take care of work arrangements with Sally and Doris Emerson. She would also have to try to explain her decision to her mother and father in a way that would not make them feel she was abandoning them.

She stayed at the desk until the lunch rush was over, then went quickly to her room. Perhaps she should tell them a fib, she thought as she started removing clothes from the hangers. Maybe she should tell them Mr. Hartstone had phoned *her*, and she could not jeopardize her job by refusing to go into the city. No. She would not lie. She was doing what she felt was best for everyone. If her motives were honorable, surely she could make her parents see the logic of her thinking. But before she discussed the subject with them, she must do something even more urgent.

She sat down at the small maple desk, took out a box of stationery, and began carefully composing a letter. She agonized over the wording for more than an hour, but at last achieved a final version that she felt hit the proper note between aloofness and self-pity.

"My dearest Rod,
I'm sorry everything has happened so suddenly

that I don't have a chance to explain to you in person. My father and I have had an unhappy difference of opinion. As you know, he is not in the best of health, and I believe it wisest if I leave Nantucket for at least a short time rather than stay here and be an unsettling influence.

By coincidence I am needed back on my television show. So it all really works out very well.

I am leaving your ring. I feel maybe we both need more time to consider our plans. I would not want you to feel you had been rushed into a commitment before you were truly ready.

> My love to you,
> Melissa

She read and reread the letter, hoping it did not sound melodramatic. She had tried to keep it as brief and matter-of-fact as possible. But it did sound awfully final, and she did not mean it to be. Absorbed in her thoughts, she gnawed the end of her pen, then added a brief postscript: "I plan to return within a week or so."

There. That left the door open. She hoped her father would have ironed things out with Rod by the time she got back. And in returning Rod's ring, she left him free to pursue his dalliance with Amelia Harding if that was what he should choose to do. For her part, she would have a grace period in which to get away and sort out the confusing complications that had piled one upon the other.

At about three she went into the sitting room to explain her plans to Paul and Ellen. Her father was working on the accounting books; her mother was drying summer wild flowers.

"I'm glad I found you both together," she began hesitantly.

"Why?" her mother asked, making an effort to keep the conversation light. "Are you about to drop some kind of bombshell? Your voice sounds as though you have something really portentous to say."

"I'm going to have to go back to New York. I'm needed back on the job." *There,* she thought. She hadn't lied; she had simply not gone into specifics. "I won't be gone long, probably only a week or two. I spoke to Sally and I don't think there'll be any problem at all with running the kitchen, Dad. She'll make out the menus and let you check them. Mother,"—she took the box holding the ring from her pocket—"I want you to give this to Rod when he comes back, please. I don't want to just leave it in his room. However, I did leave an envelope for him there, so you might check to be sure he gets it."

Her mother took the ring with a deeply puzzled frown. She stared at the box, then at Melissa, but perhaps something in the girl's expression discouraged Ellen from questioning her daughter.

"There's a plane this afternoon at about six. I'm going to take it so I can get settled in before I have to be at work on Monday. I've called a cab; it's going to pick me up at five." Her mother started to protest, but Melissa continued quickly: "I don't want you to drive me to the airport, Mother. That's the beginning of the dinner hour and you'll have your hands full. I'd rather just take a cab."

Her mother fell silent, and her father offered no comment. If he found her arrangements precipitate or odd, he did not say so. The fact that he was so willing to let her go reinforced Melissa's conviction that she was doing the right thing.

By the time she had tossed the last-minute incidentals into her suitcase, the cab was almost due to arrive. She felt she had handled the situation rather well. She had explained sufficiently, but she had tried not to burden them with a lot of unnecessary worries. She herself would have to cope with her problem with Rod at some later time.

The flight was extremely smooth and uneventful, the atmosphere unusually clear. Considering that fog was

115

more often the rule than the exception, Melissa thought herself lucky to have chosen such a flawless day. And her mood, oddly enough, was almost as serene as the weather. As the plane lifted she looked out the window and saw the tiny island become a smaller and smaller speck in the limitless dusky ocean. As it disappeared to nothingness she suddenly became aware that tears were streaming down her cheeks. It was not until that instant that she realized she had been denying her true emotions. She sank back into the upholstered seat and reveled in the luxury of giving in, at last, to her misery.

On Saturday she stocked up on a few staples and then desultorily glanced over Monday's script. Mr. Hartstone was right; it was a very light day for her. She really had only to stand against a white backdrop in a diaphanous flowing gown as she was seen in her husband's memory. She wished she had had long lines to learn—it would have given her something to do over the long weekend looming ahead.

The time dragged interminably. On Sunday afternoon she cleaned her apartment from one end to the other, although it actually needed nothing more than a dusting. But it was good to be with her motley furnishings again, most of them collected from thrift shops before she had gotten the television job. She had chosen each inexpensive item carefully, and she found them still appealing. There was the high-backed wicker chair she had bought before antique wicker became fashionable; the low oriental trunk she used as a coffee table; the drop-leaf table in the foyer that she had picked up for almost nothing and refinished herself.

She decided to go through her fall clothes and review which items she should discard and which ones needed cleaning or altering. But after half an hour of rummaging through the closet, she gave up. She could not cope with even the simple matter of dividing her clothes into separate groups; her thinking was too muddled. She thought of going to a movie but looked out the window and rejected that idea—the heat rose almost palpably from the street outside.

She considered calling three or four of her friends and inviting them over for an impromptu supper; it was one of her favorite ways of entertaining. But it would have involved answering too many questions that she didn't feel like going into at the moment. Next week, after she got back in the groove at work and had a chance to readapt to her routine, she would get in touch with the few people she really wanted to see.

She picked up a book she had left half read when she went to Nantucket, but found it impossible to become involved in it again. The characters seemed remote and uninteresting. The room was abnormally quiet. Although it was in the middle of Manhattan, her apartment building was tucked away on a street in the West Twenties that got very little traffic, particularly on a Sunday afternoon. From far down the street she could hear the distant shouts of children in the playground at the end of the block; otherwise, an oppressive silence lay over the area, a silence that was distracting by its very density.

The ring of the telephone made her start violently. As she went to pick it up she thought with a faint shrug of amusement that her nerves must be badly on edge for the phone to make her practically jump out of her skin. It must be Mr. Hartstone, for no one else knew she was in town. Unless it was Hugh Langley, the actor who played her husband on the program; perhaps he had heard of her arrival and wanted to talk to her about their scene together.

When she answered with a breathy hello, she heard a long exhalation of breath and then the impatient voice of Rod Wilshire.

"Melissa! What in God's name is going on with you?"

Her reaction was totally irrational, but the initial feeling

117

that surged through her was one of anger. Why was his first sentence almost an accusation, as though he had nothing to do with anything?

"What do you mean, Rod?" she asked carefully.

"I mean I was called in to New York for a Friday morning conference with my boss before he flew off to South America, and when I get back to Nantucket, you've flown the coop."

Flown the coop! She thought she had been very conscientious in taking care of loose ends before she left.

"But I—didn't you get my note?"

He laughed sourly. "Oh, I got your note all right. I also got your ring, thank you very much. Your mother is as bewildered by all this as I am. What's wrong with you, anyway?"

He was putting her unfairly on the defensive. Her temper flared, but she ran a hand roughly through her hair, trying to take her anger out on something more or less inanimate.

She decided to try a slight change of subject. "Did you and my father have a talk?"

"Your father? No, I haven't seen Paul since I got in. I believe he's out sailing. Why do you ask that?"

"Because—because I know he wanted to talk with you."

"What about?"

"Well, I'd rather he did the talking."

"All right." Again that tone of impatience. "But be that as it may, how long are you going to be away from here?"

She felt as though she were under cross-examination. She bit her lip. "I think not more than a week or two, as I said in the note, I believe." She was dismayed as she heard the sarcasm in her own voice. She had not meant to sound that way. On the other end there was silence. Had she angered him?

Then he gave another sigh and said, "Just stay where you are for the moment, okay?"

"Why—what do you mean?"

"I'm going to hang up. Then I'm going to find out if there's another plane back to New York tonight."

"Wait a minute, Rod. Don't do that. You just got there. Even if there is a flight, how will you get back in time for work tomorrow?"

"I'll take a train at four in the morning if I have to. We've got to get this straightened out. Just sit tight. I'll call you right back."

When the line was disconnected, she sat motionless, hunched over the telephone, propping her forehead against her hand. She could not think straight. She only knew their conversation had been frustratingly antagonistic when all she really wanted to do was to tell Rod how much she loved him.

She waited by the phone for almost an hour before she gave up and went despondently into the kitchen to make herself a cup of tea. She was dunking the tea bag up and down to strengthen the brew when the peal of the telephone again shattered the waiting stillness. She set the cup down jarringly on the cabinet and ran to answer. Before he could get out a syllable, she must make him understand her love for him had not faltered.

"Rod? I—"

"Melissa, this is a mess. Sorry, I won't be coming back to New York. Just after I hung up from talking to you, your dad came in and cornered me. I never got a chance to find out about plane schedules because he's obviously very angry with me and suspects me of acting in all sorts of devious and nefarious ways. I'm afraid I'm going to be spending the evening trying to find another room somewhere. It seems I'm no longer welcome at Highcliffe Inn."

Chapter 13

On Monday morning Melissa awoke from a fitful sleep a few minutes before the alarm went off. It was six thirty; her reporting time at the studio was eight o'clock. She climbed out of bed like an automaton and put on coffee. She was standing in front of the stove, waiting for the water to boil so she could pour it into the dripolator, when the memory of last night's conversation with Rod came back to her with stunning force.

He had told her he was moving out of Highcliffe Inn and would let her know his new address as soon as he was able to find a room. He had told her again how distressed he was by her return of the engagement ring; he would insist she take it back as soon as he saw her. At that point in the conversation it was on the tip of Melissa's tongue to introduce the subject of Amelia Harding. But some instinct told her it was the wrong time—it was not a thing to be discussed over the telephone. Through most of the talk she maintained a rather numb silence. Too much was happening too fast, and she didn't understand any of it.

But there was one thing she must find out before he hung up. "Rod," she asked, "it isn't true your crew was working off Dionis Beach, is it? I mean, you had told me you were on the other side of the island."

There was a long pause. At length he said slowly, as if weighing each word, "Melissa, I didn't lie to you. But I can't go into any further explanation. That's what I told your father, and I suppose that was what made him angrier than ever. But you'll have to take me on trust at least for a little while, darling. Please do that." There was another hesitation before he added, "I'd fly back to you tomorrow except we're—we're entering a rather delicate stage of operations. I just can't leave without, er, jeopardizing the whole expedition. That's all I can say now, Melissa. Good-bye."

As she drank the coffee Melissa acknowledged unhappily that the situation was more confusing than ever. She got dressed, hailed a cab to the studio on East Sixty-seventh Street, and walked in with a feeling of blessed relief, knowing that the next few hours would keep her mind at least partly occupied.

The white-haired doorman sitting behind the entrance desk with the morning newspaper and a cardboard container of coffee greeted her with cheery surprise. "Miss Starbuck! Didn't know you were going to be with us again so soon. Good to see you."

"Thanks, Mike. Nice to be back." She pressed the elevator button, then suddenly remembered. "Oh, how'd your daughter's wedding turn out? Was it beautiful?"

He made a triumphant circle of his thumb and forefinger. "Like clockwork. Most beautiful wedding I ever saw."

Melissa laughed as the elevator doors opened. "And of course you wouldn't be prejudiced!"

Wonderful group of people she worked with, she thought gratefully. Maybe the cheerful front she was determined to present to the world all day wouldn't have to be entirely feigned.

Her co-actors were standing about having coffee and pastry and mumbling their lines. Most of them had been called for seven thirty. They greeted Melissa effusively, told her she was crazy to have volunteered to come back to such a heat-plagued city, and made her feel generally and warmly welcome.

Hugh Langley sidled up to her and muttered with a

pseudo-wicked leer, "Glad to have you back, Lissa. It's tough being without a wife all summer."

They went through a rough blocking of the program and ran it once more, the director making a few minor line changes. Then they broke for an early lunch. After lunch the actors would have their hair and makeup done, listen to the director's notes, go through a dress rehearsal, and finally, at three, tape the show. The taping would be done in an unbroken half-hour sequence, barring a major catastrophe, just as it would eventually be aired a week later.

Melissa was dawdling over toast and coffee in a neighborhood coffee shop when Hugh Langley came in and slid into the booth opposite her. He was a clean-cut dark-blond man in his late twenties who had replaced another actor in the role only a few months before.

"Mind if I join you?"

"No, of course not. Glad to have the company." That was not strictly true; she had been trying to marshal her thoughts and decide whether she should create a fictitious family crisis and tell Mr. Hartstone she would have to go back to Nantucket once the day's work was over. But she managed a smile and motioned Hugh to sit down.

"How does it seem being back in the city?"

"Oh"—she shrugged—"it's sort of a culture shock, I guess. I feel like a displaced person right now, but I daresay by the end of the day I'll be back in harness."

"Everything okay with your apartment?"

"Oh, yes. Just fine."

"Good. Say, uh, would you like to go out to dinner tonight? I mean, I imagine it's a drag trying to get in groceries on such short notice."

"No, not really. I shopped on Saturday and my only problem is I think I bought much too much."

"Then I couldn't persuade you to find a nice, charming little spot somewhere and live it up for an evening? I just found out this morning they've extended my contract. Frankly, I was looking for someone to help me celebrate."

"Oh, Hugh, that's wonderful."

She was truly happy for him. It was customary on some daytime television shows to hire an actor on a provisional basis until the powers-that-be learned whether the viewing audience reacted favorably to him. It was often a nerve-wracking probationary period; she could fully empathize with his wish to celebrate.

"Yeah, you bet it is. So why don't you reconsider and go out with me?"

It was obvious she did not have plans for the evening, and she hated to give him a flat refusal. But she could not be away from the phone in case Rod called.

"Look," she said, "I'm expecting a long-distance telephone call tonight. Why don't you come up and have dinner with me instead?"

"No-o-o," he demurred, "I don't want to make you spend an evening cooking . . ."

"No trouble!" she said gaily. Indeed, she felt that having someone around would be a godsend. The thought of spending all evening in an empty apartment waiting for the sound of the telephone was ghastly. Rod had not in fact said he would call tonight—he might have trouble finding a permanent place to stay. If it turned out that he did not call, at least she would have companionship for the evening. Hugh seemed likable and sincere—why not? "I absolutely insist, in fact." She looked at her watch. "We'd better get back. I'll give you my address before we leave the studio."

After she got through hair and makeup, she joined the others assembled in the big studio to hear the director's notes. Henry Kaplan stood in the front of the half circle of actors, holding a sheaf of papers. Most of them were still in their robes; the costumes would be put on at the last minute so that they would be fresh.

"That was a pretty good run-through. However, there's a fairly major addition. Melissa, instead of having you just stand there while Hugh is remembering you, Hartstone

124

wants us to add a little dialogue to give the audience some idea of what you're thinking. Here's what I've come up with. Read it over and see how it hits you."

Melissa took the sheet of paper and saw that it was almost filled with a long soliloquy. "Hey!" she said jokingly, "you've really thrown me a curve."

Henry walked over and patted her shoulder. "You can do it, sweetheart. You're a quick study."

Melissa smiled up at him. It was true that she had always been able to learn lines rapidly, unlike some actors who were forced to resort to the TelePrompTer on the camera, which rolled off the lines as the scene progressed. She went to her dressing room and began studying the speech with determined concentration.

When they went through the dress rehearsal, Melissa had a bit of difficulty, but during the taping she began the speech and knew as it progressed that it was going very, very well. Even the stagehands paused in their duties and listened with close attention.

Melissa was telling her husband why she had left him: ". . . and when I saw you with—with *her,* it seemed my heart broke into a thousand pieces. I could not stay, for my despair would have communicated itself to you. I beg you to try to understand . . . I never intended you to think I loved you less."

When the scene was over and the cameras cut for what, in the program, would be a commercial break, the crew and other actors broke into spontaneous applause. Melissa was overwhelmed; it was the rarest kind of occurrence on the set of a television show. She finished the program—she had no other lines—and went to her dressing room. She had been more affected by the scene than she had thought; the lines she had spoken were words she would like to have said to Rod.

As she tried to get dressed in her street clothes her vision grew blurred with tears. She stood at the mirror dabbing at her eyes when she heard a brief rap on the door.

Hugh Langley entered. He looked at her face with an arched eyebrow. "Hey, what's this all about? You're not one of those Method actors who live their role, are you?"

She smiled wanly. "No, I'm just being silly. Here, let me write my address down for you. I'll see you about seven, okay?"

After two months of planning and preparing meals for as many as forty people, making dinner for Hugh Langley was a breeze. Melissa decided to serve southern fried chicken. She had learned the recipe not from her father but from her Virginia-born mother; it had been handed down in her family for generations. With it, mused Melissa, broccoli hollandaise, a green salad, and beaten biscuits. She thought that would do nicely for a summer evening's repast. For dessert, something simple: ice cream with fresh strawberries and a dollop of kirsch.

Hugh arrived a few minutes before seven and found Melissa still in her work costume—a pair of cutoff jeans and a frayed, oversized man's shirt she had confiscated from her father.

She let him in, then scooted back to the bedroom, calling to him to make himself at home and fix a drink if he liked. When she returned to the living room in a gaily colored muumuu her parents had sent her from Hawaii, she found Hugh in the kitchen opening a bottle of champagne.

"Did you bring that? I didn't even remember that you came in with a package."

"My motto, like that of the Boy Scouts, is, Be prepared." He lifted an airline bag from the foyer table and opened it to reveal three more bottles of champagne.

Melissa's eyes widened. "Are you expecting a dozen or so other people to join us?"

"I told you this was my night to howl. This stuff goes down like water anyway, don't you know."

Melissa smiled, but the idea of two people drinking four

126

bottles of champagne in an evening was not what she had in mind. Oh, well, she thought, she would serve dinner early, and Hugh would forget the champagne. She went into the kitchen to make the hollandaise sauce, and Hugh followed her. She wished he would settle in the living room; she was not one of those people who could cook and carry on a conversation at the same time.

"What was bothering you, Lissa, earlier today?"

She kept her concentration on the melting butter. "You mean when you found me weeping in my dressing room like a—like a dying swan?" She attempted a laugh. "Nothing. Probably delayed jet lag."

Hugh shrugged. "All right, if you don't want to level with me. I just wanted to volunteer a shoulder for you to cry on."

"Thanks, Hugh," she murmured, trying to remember whether she had put in two pats of butter or three. "Uh, would you bring me my glass from the coffee table, please?"

"Sure thing." He wandered out and returned with both their glasses refilled.

Melissa took a small sip and said, "Um, that's good. Would you mind taking the chicken in for me now?"

The dinner was delicious, Melissa thought. But Hugh concentrated more on refilling his glass of champagne than partaking of more solid nourishment. By the time she served dessert, he had opened the third bottle and become quite belligerent—not toward her but toward the director of *To Dare to Live*.

"He kept me sweating for three solid months—do you realize that?" Hugh punctuated the question by striking the end of his knife against the edge of the table.

"Oh, wait a minute, Hugh. You can't blame all that on Henry. The producer and upstairs brass all have their say, too." She did not like the tenor of his mood. Since they sat down to dine, it had changed from one of festive celebration to one of hostility. She did not want to be overtly unpleasant—she had to keep working with him. But she was dismayed by his increasing ill humor.

She was looking for a way to divert him to another topic when the downstairs buzzer rang. She looked at Hugh blankly. "That's funny. I'm not expecting anyone else." Normally in New York one did not drop by without a prior telephone call to be sure it was convenient to do so—especially since she had arrived in town so suddenly and so recently.

She pressed the intercom. "Who is it?"

The voice was muffled, but it seemed to be something about a package. She pushed the buzzer, which would open the front door, and turned back to Hugh. "It's a package delivery, I think. Maybe a messenger with the rest of this week's scripts. Ordinarily I don't buzz people in unless I know exactly who it is. But with you here to protect me, I guess there's nothing to worry about."

Hugh smiled with an air of braggadocio. "You're damn right."

She heard the elevator ascend, then it stopped. After a moment there was a firm, staccato knock on the hallway door. She opened the peephole, which afforded a view into the corridor. Through the tiny slot she could see the haggard face of Rod Wilshire.

Chapter 14

Rod strode into the apartment and stopped dead in his tracks when he saw Hugh Langley. Hugh got up from the table slowly and walked over to Rod, an empty grin on his face.

"You the fella who's been giving my wife a hard time?" he asked in the confident tone of a master comedian making a priceless witticism.

Melissa glared at him, then turned her attention back to Rod. He was in chinos and a sweatshirt, and he looked very tired.

"What is that supposed to mean?" Rod asked without amusement.

Melissa, trying to smooth the matter over, gave a half-hearted laugh. "Hugh Langley, Rod Wilshire. Hugh plays my husband on the TV show, Rod. He's just trying to be funny. Pay no attention to him." She paused for a long moment, then indicated a chair. "Please. Sit down and I'll bring you some coffee or a drink or something."

Rod remained standing. "I don't know that I should intrude. You two seem to be having such a cozy tête-à-tête."

"Please," she implored him *sotto voce,* "don't add to my troubles."

He looked at her briefly with wry amusement. Hugh had fetched the bottle of champagne and was waving it in Rod's face. "Let us not trifle with inferior beverages.

Drink of the elixir of the gods. Melissa, a glass for the noble lord.''

Cringing, yet also feeling a strange urge to giggle wildly, Melissa got a glass from the cupboard. Hugh poured Rod's drink with a great flourish, then raised his own. "To your health, m'lord." He gave a low bow, recovering his equilibrium with some difficulty.

Melissa felt she had somehow become caught in the middle of a comic opera. But when she flicked a glance at Rod, she saw that his amusement had disappeared and the muscles around his mouth were tight.

Hugh insisted on opening the final bottle of champagne and dispensing it among them. His mood had swung once again from geniality to sullenness. "I asked you a question when you first came in, m'lord, and you did not deign to answer it." He addressed Rod insinuatingly.

"And what was that?" Rod was trying to conceal his impatience with the younger man.

"Are you the blackguard who's been making life miserable for my darling devoted wife?"

Melissa squirmed in her chair. She was sure Rod was not taking Hugh seriously, but it was an idiotic situation. She longed for Hugh to beat a hasty and diplomatic retreat. She and Rod had so much to talk about. He looked worn-out; he must have left Nantucket immediately after his day of work.

"Your darling devoted *wife*, as you put it, is the one who deserted me, not vice versa." Rod made a valiant effort to keep his voice light.

"Not according to the tales I've been hearing."

"Hugh!" Suddenly Melissa was really angry; she had humored her tipsy guest quite long enough. "Please just leave. You're becoming very tiresome and I—"

Rod broke in smoothly. "No, Melissa, on the contrary, this is getting very interesting." He turned from her to Hugh. "Tell me about some of the tales you've been hearing. I'm all ears."

Melissa's anger expanded to include Rod among its targets. Surely he must see that Hugh's pointless joking was only an effect of the alcohol he had consumed. Why encourage the man?

Hugh winked at Rod knowingly. "She's told me plenty. And I don't approve of your despicable behavior one bit."

With one lithe pouncing movement—so swift Melissa hardly saw it—Rod pulled Hugh out of his chair by the collar of his shirt. "I asked you to tell me all about it," he said, his voice dangerously soft. "So talk."

Instantly the pendulum of Hugh's emotions swung to another extreme. He became a cowering, helpless little boy begging for mercy. "Ah, come on, I'm only kidding you. For Pete's sake, can't you take a joke?"

"I'm not especially in the mood for jokes right now, Hugh. So why don't you run along?"

Melissa sat in embarrassed silence while Hugh gathered his belongings. When she opened the door for him, he grinned weakly as he muttered, "Your friend seems to be the anti-social sort. But thanks for the dinner." She pressed the elevator button for him and waited until the doors slid open.

"Good night, Hugh. I'll see you tomorrow."

When she reentered the room, Rod was standing at the bookcase. He had taken down a copy of *Eight Greek Tragedies*, a textbook Melissa had used in college.

"When I was in Greece last summer, I saw *Medea* at the amphitheater in Epidaurus," he observed evenly. "It was quite a wonderful experience."

He sounded like a polite guest who was nothing more than a casual acquaintance.

"Oh, Rod," she said, feeling helplessly that the mood of the evening was already askew. "Did you have to be so—so physical with poor Hugh? He was just being what he mistakenly thought was funny."

Rod laid the book aside and took her hand gravely. She

131

felt the familiar weakness in her legs as his warm, throbbing fingers clasped hers.

"Melissa, my love, I flew to New York to see you, and I have to get a very early train back to Woods Hole tomorrow morning. I didn't mean to be unkind to your friend; but, on the other hand, I had no intention of sitting here all evening with a third party, especially one who seemed intent on making inane insinuations."

She looked at him searchingly, as if seeking reassurance that his feelings for her were as steadfast as hers for him. He met her gaze unflinchingly.

"Let's sit down, Rod," she said softly, "and see if we can get all this sorted out."

She knew from the beginning he would tell her no more about his work, so she asked no questions. She gathered from his general demeanor that Paul Starbuck was seriously upset with him, though Rod went into no details. And she did not question him about it; she would wait until she returned to Nantucket, then have a long talk with her father.

"Where are you staying, Rod? In Nantucket, I mean."

"I found a place in 'Sconset. It's very nice—right on the ocean. Although I must admit I do miss Highcliffe Inn."

"Where are the others on your crew? I mean, did Dad ask them all to find another place?"

She could not quite decipher the expression that crossed his face. His eyes darkened and for an instant he looked quite angry. Then he regained his former composure.

"Jerry and Jim Wilson are no longer with the crew. Bob Converse and Les Hylton are both in 'Sconset with me. Two new men came up to take the Wilsons' place—they're there, too."

Melissa's mind moved to another subject. She wanted desperately to ask him about Amelia Harding, but she did not know how to introduce the topic. Obviously he was not totally engrossed in the attractive librarian, or he would not be sitting in her living room at this moment.

Then it struck Melissa that Rod did not even know of her suspicions. He had no idea that he and Amelia had been seen that day at the Crown and Coronet. Wouldn't it be only fair to give him a chance to explain? She was being as rash in prejudging him as she had accused her father of being.

She cleared her throat and raised her eyes to his. "Rod, I guess you thought it odd of me to return your ring—"

"Odd!" He exploded with anger. "You little fool, I thought you had taken leave of your senses. Which reminds me." He went to the foyer closet where she had hung his light jacket, and dug into its pocket. "Put this back on and promise me you'll never be so asinine again."

There was nothing she wanted more than to slip that token of his love back on her finger. But the thing with Amelia had to be cleared up before she could accept it again. "Wait, Rod. I must tell you something . . . I must tell you why I left it with Mother to give back to you." She coughed nervously. She wished she had not touched the champagne; she needed a completely lucid mind in order to choose her next phrases carefully. "You see, the day I left Nantucket—well, that was the day you left, too"—she blinked with confusion as she realized it had been only three days ago; it seemed a year at the very least—"but one of the reasons for my leaving was that I went to the library that afternoon and found it temporarily closed. To while away the ten minutes or so that I had to wait for it to open again, I wandered down a little hidden lane. I discovered a garden cocktail lounge, a place I never knew existed before that day. It looked rather intriguing, so I peeked through the—"

Slowly dawning comprehension began to break over Rod's face. "Wait a minute. Are you going to tell me you returned my ring and left Nantucket because you saw me with Amelia Harding?" He was incredulous. "I can't believe even you would be that obtuse." He shook his head helplessly.

133

Melissa knew he was joking, but her temper rose. "Maybe I am obtuse, but when I see a man and a woman holding hands in a secluded garden and gazing into each other's eyes like lovesick calves, what am I supposed to think?"

"Lissa, please, just calm down for a second. Amelia had gotten word that morning that her older sister was seriously ill and in a hospital somewhere in Minnesota. She was to be operated on the next day. I happened to go into the library, and seeing how distraught Amelia was, I insisted that she go with me for a drink. We were not 'holding hands' in any romantic way. I was merely trying to offer her what comfort I could. I knew someone who had had a similar operation, so I think I was able to make her feel a bit better. That's all there was to it. If you had just asked me for an explanation, my explosive little redhead, the whole thing could have been cleared up in thirty seconds."

Melissa began to feel idiotic, but she also felt compelled to explain the reasons for her seeming foolishness. "But, Rod, it was just that everything happened at once. Dad and I had had an argument about your working off Dionis Beach when you had assured me the work was on the other side of the island. Then I saw you with Amelia. And then, of course, I remembered what Benny had said—"

"What Benny had said? What in God's name was that?"

She repeated the remark Benny had overheard the night of the clambake, about Rod's having camped on Amelia's doorstep. "It did sound incriminating, you have to admit . . ."

Rod strode over to her and took her in his arms almost roughly. "You little fool. Couldn't you figure out what I meant when I said that? I didn't mean I had been pursuing the woman or camping on the doorstep of her *home.* I had been camping on the doorstep of the library, for God's sake! I had to do a lot of research before I started the job, and the maps and charts I needed were available only in

134

the Nantucket library. It wasn't a question of data that I could assemble elsewhere and take with me."

She looked at his weary open face and could not doubt his honesty. Pricked by remorse, she lifted her hands and let her palms slide tenderly down his cheeks. "Oh, Rod, I guess I've been an awful fool."

"I think that's the understatement of the century. Now will you recover your senses and put this ring back where it belongs?"

He reached for her hand and slipped the ring back on the proper finger. Impulsively she caught his hand and searched the back of it, looking at the long brown fingers, the small tufts of black hair between the knuckles. The dark masculine hair was very exciting to her; she drew his hand to her mouth and touched it with her lips, then raised her eyes to meet his burning gaze.

"What time is it?" he asked hoarsely.

She glanced at her watch, not believing its reading. "Eleven!"

"Can't be." He looked at his own watch and shook his head. "God. I thought it was about nine."

"What time's your train tomorrow?"

He groaned. "Would you believe five thirty?" He stretched his shoulders, sighed, and pulled her down beside him onto the overstuffed cushions at one end of the sofa. "Darling Melissa," he murmured, "when are we ever going to have all the time we need for me to show you how much I love you? We're together—alone—and I have to worry about dashing out at the break of dawn to catch a train. You have to worry about being at the studio bright-eyed and bushy-tailed. I want to make love to you, and yet, I don't want it to end with a mad dash on both our parts to get out and face the workaday world. It's a hell of a—"

He was lying with his head in her lap, and she put a finger gently over his lips. "I know, Rod. I feel the same way. The first time we make love, I want it to be out of

135

The Arabian Nights. I want little slave girls to anoint my feet and perfume my hair. I want torchlights flickering. I want strange exotic music. I want pomegranates and huge golden bowls of luscious fruit. I want couches draped in oriental brocades—"

"And we can try them all?" He raised an eyebrow and grinned roguishly.

She sighed in mock annoyance. "You sure know how to stifle a girl's imagination. I was just getting started."

"C'mere." His voice was sandpapery with desire as he reached for her imperiously and pulled her down to him. He kissed her hungrily as if he could never get enough of the taste of her; her falling curtain of flaming hair covered his face and eyes. The blood rushed to her head; she could feel a tiny pulse beating frantically in her temple. His mouth moved away from hers and slid to the hollow at the base of her throat. She stretched onto the cushion beside him, and he adjusted his body so that his face was now above hers. In the lamplight his eyes were shadowed by their thick, spiky lashes, but she could read their unmistakable message of desire.

"I love you, Rod. Forever and ever."

"And I you," he answered, as if in incantation. "Till the end of time."

His hand reached for the top button of her shirt and opened it. When she felt his fingers on her naked breast, she sucked in her breath sharply. It was the first time he had touched those breasts directly, without intervening fabric. She placed her hand over his and pushed his fingers into the softness. From deep in the center of her being an urgent need throbbed and swirled, making her feel lightheaded. She felt his tongue gently circling her nipples, then brushing, tasting, one after the other. She raised her hand to caress the back of his head and felt the soft short tendrils behind his ears.

When the telephone shrilled, she thought for a moment it was the mad ringing of her own brain. She opened her

136

eyes and glanced around dazedly, then went shakily to answer it.

Evan Hartstone's voice was full of apology. "Sorry to call so late, Melissa. But I've just been doing the final blocking on tomorrow's show, and I think it'll work better if we use you right at the beginning, in the teaser. So could you make it half an hour earlier than scheduled? I'd appreciate it."

Melissa grimaced at Rod but kept her voice determinedly cheerful. "I'll be there, Mr. Hartstone. No problem."

She walked back over to where Rod sat, his look questioning. She gazed down at him resignedly. "Would you like a cup of coffee? It'll keep us awake long enough to watch the dawn."

They did not watch the dawn, for both fell asleep in each other's arms like two exhausted children. At four thirty Rod roused himself from the brief, fitful sleep, shaved hastily, and gulped the steaming coffee Melissa had ready for him.

"I hope you won't fall asleep twenty fathoms down and forget to breathe."

"At least I don't have to face the all-seeing eye of the camera."

Her laugh sounded forced in spite of her best acting efforts. "Oh, the makeup man is a wizard. I'll be fine." Her laughter faded. "I just wish this hadn't been such a miserably short time."

He put his mug down, his mood thoughtful. "What are you doing this weekend? I mean, do you have to stay in New York another week?" She nodded. "Why don't I fly down on Friday when we can have the whole weekend together?"

"Super! Sheer heaven," she answered. Then she glanced nervously at her watch. "Now get out of here before you miss that train."

When the Air New England plane taxied down the

runway the next Friday afternoon, Melissa thought her heart would surely leap from her body. The prospect of two days with Rod stretched before her like a luxurious infinity.

He looked quite different from the way he had appeared on Monday. Today he wore a tan linen sport jacket and dark brown trousers. She devoured him with her eyes. He was beautiful; there was no other word to describe him. When he caught sight of her, he broke into a run, pulled her off the ground, and swung her in a circle high in the air.

"Rod!" she cried through her laughter. "Stop it! People will think we're totally insane."

"Well, aren't we?"

"Of course we are. But don't let it get around."

He set her down and enveloped her in his arms. Melissa could feel the beat of his heart; her own answered with a demented flutter. He held her at arms' length and drank in the sight of her thirstily. "You look terrific." His eyes skimmed the softly clinging green jersey dress. "On you that color is so wicked you're a menace to society."

"You fool," she teased softly. "Do we need to go to baggage claim?"

"Nope. It's all here." He indicated the carry-on duffel bag.

"Is that the famous duffel bag that ran into my bike that first day?"

"Of course not, idiot. How could any mere duffel bag survive an assault like that? Oh, no, that victim of your recklessness had to be scrapped. This is its replacement. If I'd had my wits about me, I'd have sent you a bill."

In the cab he wiped a hand across his forehead. "It's hot as blazes, isn't it?"

"I know a place where we can cool off," she said with sudden inspiration. She directed the driver to the Battery, at the south end of the island, where they took a Staten Island ferry. The lights of the magnificent city glowed

138

behind the stubby boat-like jewels. It was that bewitching hour of midsummer dusk when the sky turns a deep and velvety blue and the world seems suspended in a state of unreal beauty. To their right the Statue of Liberty, majestic arm upraised, glimmered out of the darkening sky.

The air on the water was cool and damp. They stood side by side at the railing and watched the city lights slowly recede as the sturdy little boat chugged across the bay. They returned to Manhattan an hour later, cooled and refreshed, and walked through the Wall Street area to a restaurant Rod knew about in Chinatown. The food arrived in minutes looking delectable: lobster in black bean sauce, and beef with walnuts and hot peppers. They cooled the delicious fieriness with Chinese beer.

Back in her apartment, Melissa played a new record album for Rod. They began to dance to the insinuatingly sensuous sound of Andrés Segovia's classical Spanish guitar, circling the room slowly, lazily. The record ended; they stood quietly in each other's arms. This was the moment she had been waiting for, yet she was nervous and uncertain. She felt the way she did before an important audition. Silly.

"Well," he said, "here we are at last."

"Yes," she echoed. "Here we are." She moved away awkwardly and sat down at one end of the sofa.

"What's the matter, Lissa?"

She frowned and tried to frame a logical reply.

Rod looked at her intently. "Is it your father?"

She cupped her chin in her hand. "Yes. Yes, I suppose it is. I don't like to think of things as being less than perfect—between him and me, between him and you." She stole a sidewise glance at Rod's profile. "Foolish of me, isn't it?"

Standing above her, he tousled the thick mane of scarlet hair. "I want you to do something, Lissa." She looked up at him. "I want you to trust me." His voice had never been so soft, so loving. "Take it on trust that when my job in

139

Nantucket's over, your father and I won't have any more problems."

Something in his tone imbued her with total faith; her nervousness evaporated and was replaced by wild excitement. She rose and put her arms about him fiercely. "Oh, Rod, I do trust you. Truly I do."

His own arms enclosed her. He drew in a sharp breath and pulled her to the sofa. He pushed her gently against the cushions, and his fingers explored her face, outlining her mouth, her eyes, her cheek, as though he could not fully believe the wonder of her. Their eyes were locked—his tender, yet full of desire; hers waiting, trusting, unafraid.

Again his move, when it came, was lithe and sudden. He bent over her, and her world narrowed in an instant to the feel of his mouth on hers. She answered his questing tongue with equal eagerness. Her body was on fire. She could feel her nipples tighten almost painfully as the hard musculature of his body weighted itself upon hers.

"Should I turn out the lights?" she whispered. She was suddenly shy in the presence of his overwhelming, demanding masculinity.

"No, please." He stayed her outstretched hand. "I want to see you. I love you, Melissa."

She was drowning in a cocoon of warm liquid. She wanted to speak, to tell Rod that his love for her was given back to him a thousandfold, but the myriad delicious sensations that assaulted her body were so all-consuming she could find no words. She gave herself up to them, reveling in the heaviness of his hard body against her. An ecstatic gasp escaped her as his hand, in feathery-light caressing exploration, moved slowly over her belly to the inside of her thigh.

She lazily put her arms around his shoulders, looked up at him, and smiled. She felt wonderfully relaxed and replete. He looked at her and brushed her curving lips tenderly with his fingers.

"You're wonderful, Lissa."

"We're both wonderful. Don't say any more. There's no need." She smiled again, thinking how primitive a form of communication words really were.

"You look like a Cheshire cat," he said.

"Why?" She feigned indignation.

"So smug and self-satisfied." Laughter lurked at the corners of his mouth.

She gave him a mock jab in the chest. "I just feel so happy."

"No regrets?"

"None—ever."

He bent to kiss her. She felt a stab of arousal, but this time it was accompanied by a fierce pride of possession. Rod belonged to her. She thought, *I'll have to keep pinching myself for days to come. This glorious man is mine.*

"What's the grin for?" he asked, pushing a lock of hair away from her face.

"Let a girl have a few secrets, will you?"

He kissed the tip of her nose. "As long as they make you smile."

"I've always loved your eyebrows, did you know that?" She traced their outlines with the tips of her fingers. "They're—I don't know—honest."

The crooked grin flashed. "Oh, ho. So you're not in love with me at all, you're in love with my honest eyebrows."

"That's about the size of it." She smiled and started to embrace him again.

"I have to leave," he said softly.

"Wha—what?" She thought she must have misunderstood his words.

He began to dress rapidly and efficiently. "I'm sorry, Lissa, I have to go. I should have told you sooner. My boss is calling me early tomorrow before he takes off on a two-week trip to Egypt."

"Oh, Rod—" She cut off her words. Rod knew what his job responsibilities were; she would not make him feel guilty by playing the role of abandoned martyr.

"I'll call you tomorrow about noon," he promised. "Get some rest—you've had a busy week."

She nodded, keeping her head lowered so that he would not see the shadow of hurt on her face.

He pulled her to him and kissed her gently and hastily. "Love you." And he was gone.

She turned back into the room. The record had long since finished, but the On light of the stereo still glowed. She clicked it off and looked around the room blankly. The silence was deafening.

Chapter 15

Rod called a few minutes after twelve on Saturday.

"Come on over," Melissa invited gaily. "I'll make you brunch."

After a pause he said, "That sounds like a lovely idea, but a—a business appointment has come up. I'm not going to be able to make it till later this afternoon."

"Not even if I promise to produce the best eggs Benedict you ever tasted?"

"No. Sorry, darling. I'll see you about four if that's okay with you."

"Well, of course, if it can't be helped. But I was hoping —I thought we might be lucky enough to get some last-minute matinee tickets for whatever you wanted to see."

"Yes. Well, I'll see you about four."

"Okay."

She hung up, feeling suddenly at loose ends. Four hours before she would see him. Four hours before he would hold her in his arms. It was a lifetime. *Oh, stop it, you mopey calf,* she told herself sharply. *Do something constructive.*

She decided to cook something spectacular. Tonight they were going to Windows on the World for dinner, but she could make a treat for Sunday brunch. She got down her favorite cookbook and began leafing through it. She found a recipe for a chocolate-orange *gâteau* that sounded delicious and looked complicated enough to consume at least four hours. She rushed to the grocery store for the additional items she needed: semisweet chocolate, oranges, heavy cream, and sweet butter.

By the time she smoothed on the last spoonful of icing and garnished the cake with lacy curlings of orange peel, it was almost three thirty. But the hours of work had been worth it; the *gâteau,* its layers filled with brandy-flavored whipped cream, did look truly impressive. Perhaps she could give her father competition in the kitchen, after all!

She hurried into the bedroom to change her clothes. She would not dress for dinner yet; they could amble through Chelsea before honoring their restaurant reservations at seven o'clock. She had barely pulled a white cotton sweater over her pink denim pants when Rod arrived.

"How did your business appointment go?" Her voice was lilting with happiness; she was trying to decide whether to show Rod the *gâteau* now or keep it as a Sunday surprise.

"Oh—fine. Would you like to take a walk somewhere?"

She raised herself on tiptoe to kiss him. "Just what I had in mind."

As they browsed through Chelsea's antique shops and stopped in a tiny restaurant for a glass of iced tea, it occurred to her that Rod seemed unusually quiet.

"Is something bothering you, Rod?" she asked at last.

He answered with that heart-melting lopsided smile. "Of course not. I guess I'm just a little weary. I had a rather full week myself."

She smiled and nodded sympathetically and put the matter out of her mind.

They stopped again briefly at her apartment, where she changed into a simple, clinging black jersey, demurely high-necked in front but swooping almost to her waist in back. When she emerged from the bedroom, Rod took one look at her and went into a mock swoon.

"I shouldn't have been calling you tiny mite. *Dyna*mite would be more like it."

"Corny joke!" she chided to hide her inordinate pleasure at his compliment.

He moved behind her and kissed her bare shoulder. His lips progressed leisurely down her naked back. "Are you sure those reservations are for seven?" he asked huskily.

The sensation of his lips on her back was drawing her into light-headed desire. With more willpower than she knew she possessed, she gently disentangled his laced fingers from around her waist. "I'm certain, my darling. Sorry."

He gave the nape of her neck a last quick nip before he surrendered with a sigh. "Till later, then," he murmured. "Dammit."

She laughed with teasing promise in her eyes.

Windows on the World surpassed its advance billing. The view from over a hundred stories high was awe-inspiring. The lights of lesser buildings rose around them like bejeweled upstretched arms. The evening was unusually clear; across the black expanse of the Hudson River the lights of New Jersey looked very near. The maitre d' seated them side by side at a low banquette, which gave both of them access to the breathtaking panorama spread before them.

Rod immediately ordered champagne. Melissa, taking her first sip after they had clinked glasses, noticed how superior it tasted to that which Hugh Langley had brought to dinner. *It isn't the difference in the champagne,* she thought. *It's the difference in the company. It's drinking it with someone you love.*

Melissa ordered soft-shell crabs, asparagus, and potato soufflé, and Rod veal *piccata* with linguine.

The low murmur of the other diners hardly intruded itself on their consciousness. It was as though they were in their own private aerie high in the sky. The food arrived. Melissa's tiny almond-studded crabs were sautéed to crisp golden perfection; Rod's veal was redolent of wine and lemon.

They were waiting for dessert and coffee when their idyll was broken, quite suddenly, by the appearance of a woman in a flaming-red dress and dangling gold earrings. She was very tall, probably only a few inches shorter than Rod, and her ebony hair was severely swept back from her face. To Melissa's stunned amazement she approached their table and whispered something in Rod's ear. He looked annoyed, and his face flushed with either anger or embarrassment—Melissa was not sure which. However, he rose politely and then stiffly introduced the two women.

"Melissa Starbuck, this is Tracy Nightingale."

Tracy bestowed on Melissa a dazzling smile, revealing small, perfect white teeth. "I do hope you'll forgive my intruding like this. But when I had lunch with Rod today, he told me the two of you were coming here tonight and I suppose, frankly, I was just overwhelmed by curiosity about you. So I persuaded my friends to bring me by for a drink—they're sitting at the bar."

While Melissa searched vainly for some reply, Tracy continued in her husky, breathy voice: "Heavens, you're a tiny little thing. Short girls are so cute. I've always envied them. Oh, by the way, Rod, while I think of it— your maroon bathrobe is still in my apartment. Maybe you'll want to come by and pick it up sometime soon." She turned to Melissa again. "Awfully nice to have met you, Miss Buck. I do hope you won't have too much trouble keeping this Don Juan under control. He does have a weakness for the ladies." She smiled brightly. "Well, I'd better rejoin my friends. Good night now." She swirled away, her scarlet skirt fluttering behind her.

Melissa looked dumbly at the lemon tart and coffee the waiter was setting before her. She could feel Rod's eyes on her, but she did not look at him or speak. There seemed to be nothing to say.

The silence continued for several agonizing moments until Rod gave a gruff *harrumph* and found his voice. "My

146

God, Melissa, I'm sorry. I wouldn't knowingly have put you through that for anything in the world."

"A business appointment." Her voice was low and bemused. She repeated the three words blankly: "A business appointment."

"Melissa, please hear me out. Tracy called me at my hotel—apparently a mutual friend had told her I was in town. She asked me if I would meet her and help her move to a new apartment—no, wait, you've got to listen. Tracy is a wonderful actress when she wants to be. She told me the landlord was turning the building into a condominium, had gotten very nasty with her about it, and she had to move immediately. . . ."

Melissa mouthed the words again, as though they constituted her entire vocabulary: "A business appointment —"

"Can't you see, sweetheart, to me it *was* just a business appointment. I was simply doing a favor for—for an old friend. But I didn't see any point in worrying you by telling you it was Tracy. When I got to her place, she told me the moving van was late, wouldn't be there for a couple of hours, and we might as well go out for lunch. That's when I called you, because I could see I had let myself in for a long-drawn-out process."

"Too bad you didn't remember to pick up your maroon bathrobe while you were there." It was hard to shape the words; her lips felt stiff. But the softness of her voice did not conceal its sarcasm.

He raised his hands as if to ward off a blow. "All right. Tracy and I lived together. But when I told you it was over, I meant it. I still do. It's over with her, too. She doesn't care about me anymore. She's just one of those creatures who's determined to make trouble if she can find a way to do it. It's a hobby with her. That's the God's truth, Melissa."

Melissa had listened to his narration with a numb, glazed expression on her face. Now she felt a dangerous

147

wave of fury rising inside her throat. She felt like screaming, like physically attacking him, like crashing the exquisite china to the floor. She struggled desperately for
control until she could get out of this public place. She
made her hands into tight fists and took a deep breath,
being careful to modulate her voice when she spoke.

"Rod, I trusted you about your work, whatever it is,
even though my father no longer believes you worthy of
trust. I believed you when you said you were merely com-
forting Amelia. I took you at your word when you said it
was over between you and Tracy Nightingale. But you
called it a business appointment when you knew you were
meeting *her*. You fell—or say you fell—for that condominium story that a six-year-old child wouldn't have
swallowed." She took a deep, ragged breath, then spat out
her final malediction: "Go to hell! Go to hell, and good-
bye!"

Choking on the final words, she picked up her handbag
from the seat of the banquette and stumbled down the long
aisle between the tables, her hand over her mouth to keep
the other diners from seeing her stricken, contorted face.

She let herself into her apartment, undressed, and went
immediately to bed. In the dark she listened to the insistent ring of the telephone. It rang for a long time, stopped,
then half an hour later began ringing again. She lay motionless, her eyes staring upward toward the invisible ceil-
ing. The phone rang five different times over the next two
hours, but after midnight it did not ring again. In the
blackness of the room the fluorescent hands of the clock
crept stealthily through the endless hours. The last time
Melissa glanced at it with sleepless, staring eyes it read five
twenty.

She was shocked out of sleep the next morning; it was
the telephone again, clamoring shrilly into her conscious
mind. She felt groggy, as though she had been drugged.
She clambered stiffly out of bed and started for the phone

148

before she remembered the previous evening. She stopped, stood rigid, and waited for the metronomic ringing to cease. She could not imagine why, but every bone in her body ached. She fell exhaustedly into bed again, but sleep eluded her. Finally, a little before noon, she dragged herself to the kitchen and made a cup of instant coffee. When she opened the refrigerator for cream, the sight of the elaborate *gâteau,* lightly covered with transparent plastic wrap, almost sickened her. She would give it to a neighbor later. Or throw it down the incinerator.

At about three that afternoon the downstairs buzzer sounded. It would surely be Rod's last attempt to contact her over the weekend, she thought dazedly. He would have to return to Nantucket, probably by the late-afternoon plane. She walked slowly toward the intercom and raised her hand to press the button. But what was there to say? She slowly let her hand drop and resumed her place in the corner of the sofa, burrowing into the softness of the cushions like a wounded animal. It must have been a full ten minutes before the buzzer stopped.

The second week in New York was a nightmare. Melissa learned her lines, played her part, behaved normally on the surface, even forcing herself to joke with her fellow actors. But it was all done in a state of numbness; an invisible gear in her head had switched to automatic.

Hugh Langley, who had apologized profusely for his behavior on that unfortunate Monday evening, asked her to go out with him again, promising his conduct would be exemplary in every way. But she refused him brusquely, not even bothering to offer an explanation.

Her last working day was Thursday, and she decided to return to Nantucket on Friday by train and ferry rather than by plane. She did not want to walk through La Guardia Airport again and be tormented by memories of her last time there, when she had gone to meet Rod's plane.

The train ride was mercifully uneventful and even relaxing. Melissa, who had had trouble sleeping during the entire week, soon found herself soothed by the monotonous grinding of the wheels against the tracks and dozed most of the way to Woods Hole. When she got to the ferry slip, she found the weather, even on the waterfront, muggy and windless. A boatload of passengers was just disembarking from Nantucket. She asked the ticket clerk how much time she had, and was told a little over half an hour. Wandering into a nearby coffee shop, she sat down in a Leatherette booth and gave her order for a lemonade to the fresh-faced waitress, probably a high-schooler making extra summer money like Doris.

She was examining the pseudo old New England decor when she happened to glance at the man passing her booth.

"Why—Jim Wilson!" she said with some surprise. "What are you doing here?"

"I'm waiting for a bus up to the Cape, to visit my family."

She motioned him to join her. "But I thought—that is, Rod said you weren't working with him any—"

"That's right. I'm not with Rod's crew anymore. I'm on a—an independent project."

He seemed nervous. Melissa was somewhat amused, surmising that perhaps he was jumpy because he was in the presence of an "older woman." He couldn't be more than twenty-one, she decided.

He continued to chatter, fidgeting with the collar of his open-necked sport shirt. "See, I was only doing the preliminary exploration and placing of the gear on that job of Rod's. The rest of whatever he's doing is too secret to let us peons in on. I think he's getting his orders straight from Washington, to tell you the truth."

"Washington? I thought his company was based in New York."

"Oceanic Surveying. Yeah, it is. But they contract for

150

jobs with different concerns, including work for the federal government."

"I see." The news, if true, was a revelation. It explained Rod's secretiveness, his stubborn refusal to confide in her about his work or to defend himself against her father's accusations that he was an unscrupulous bounty hunter. "So you're just assigned to a different project that Oceanic is doing? And your group is working off Dionis Beach?"

"Yeah. That's where we're working. But we're not with Oceanic. I can't tell you what we're digging for, but if we succeed, I can tell you this: I'll be driving a Jaguar instead of taking a bus."

Something was not quite right about his story, and Melissa could not figure out what element was askew. She took another sip of her drink, and then she remembered. Her father had said the equipment off Dionis Beach was marked "Oceanic Surveying."

"That's odd," she said. "Dad said the equipment off Dionis was Oceanic's."

Jim Wilson coughed. After a pause his voice took on a confidential inflection: "Well . . . let's say we 'borrowed' a few pieces from them. You know?"

"Yes," she said, staring straight at him. "I think I do, Jim."

His face reddened. He got up almost immediately, muttered something about being late, paid his bill, and hurried out of the coffee shop without looking back.

Melissa sat for a while in deep thought. Rod was apparently working on a secret project of some kind for the government, if Jim Wilson's surmise was correct. The group working off Dionis Beach was a piratical offshoot from Rod's original crew. They must be engaged in some kind of illegal treasure hunt. She remembered her father's mention of the *Andrea Doria*. Perhaps Jim Wilson and his crew were trying to accomplish what no one else had been able to do: conquer the treacherous currents that surrounded the sunken liner and pillage its cargo for the rumored stolen jewels.

Her conversation with Jim had convinced her of one thing: Rod had told her as much of the truth as he felt he had the moral right to disclose. She thought she now had the information she needed to defend him to her father. But would Rod want her to use it?

Chapter 16

When the ferry at last got under way, Melissa stood at the railing thinking back on the ride she and Rod had taken together on the much smaller Staten Island boat. The briny air, the motion of the wind on her cheeks, the feeling of the deck under her feet, were all reminders of that magic evening. But what a difference in her mood! The world on that night in Manhattan (was it possible it had been only a week ago?) had been rich with the promise of as much happiness as her heart could hold. On this Friday afternoon, on her way back to Nantucket, her emotions were a tangle of overwhelming confusion.

She was excited by the prospect of being back on the island: her two weeks in Manhattan had made her appreciate Nantucket's fresh country simplicity more than ever before. Yet she felt devastated that Rod would not be meeting her at Steamboat Wharf, laughing with delight as he enfolded her in his strong brown arms. She looked forward to being with her family again, yet she dreaded the awkwardness that must surely ensue if the conversation turned to Rod. And most irrational of all, in some tiny, remote corner of her mind there lurked a hope that somehow Rod would be magically restored to room 305 and that all the problems would have vanished.

She smiled ruefully at her own caprice as she realized the ferry was pulling into its slip at the wharf. She was astonished to see Benny waiting on the pier, jubilantly waving his green-visored cap in her direction.

"Benny!" she exclaimed delightedly. "I didn't expect to be met. I hadn't even told anyone exactly when I was getting here."

"Let me take that," he said, hugging her and reaching for her suitcase. "You told Mother Thursday was your last working day. I just had a premonition you might come up on the train, and since I was downtown this afternoon anyway, I decided to wait for the ferry and see if you were aboard."

"How lucky for me!" She got into the passenger's seat. "But aren't you still working at that divers' shop?"

"Yes, sure. I was just on my way home—the boss had to go up to Boston this afternoon so we closed early."

"Still like it?" she asked with interest as he drove down South Beach Street.

"It's changed my whole life," he said with rare simplicity. "You should take up diving, Liss. You'd probably be good at it."

Melissa laughed. "What makes you think so?"

"Because it's a field where lighter body weight can be an advantage."

"Maybe I'll try it someday." As an afterthought she added, "If being lightweight is an advantage, you must be a champion."

Benny responded with an uncharacteristically robust laugh.

She wanted to ask him if he had seen Rod, but she bit the words back. Why would Rod have been in touch with the Starbuck family when Paul Starbuck had vented his displeasure about Rod's work in no uncertain terms, and when Melissa herself had refused to answer the phone or open the door to him? Her feelings were ambivalent and absurd. She determinedly tried to turn off her mind.

It was late August, and the famous Nantucket roses were rampant, as though they were intent on one last fling before summer's end. They threatened to overgrow front yards, they climbed riotously over every trellis, they even

154

made progress halfway up the sides of buildings. The downtown streets were packed with camera-clicking tourists who apparently hoped their snapshots would capture the deep and vibrant scarlet and wine of the glorious flowers. Melissa knew they had set themselves an impossible task. The colors, like sunsets or rainbows, were too spectacular a phenomenon of nature ever to be transferred to film; the infinite subtlety of their shadings was too elusive.

"You seem far away, Liss. Jet lag from the ferry ride?" Benny laughed heartily at his own joke.

"Just admiring the roses, Benny." They turned onto Cliff Road. "Mother said Dad was fine when I talked to her midweek. Is he still?"

Benny grinned. "He's getting lazy. I think it's taken him till now to really wind down from the hectic pace he used to keep up in New York. I've been sailing with him once or twice." He added as an afterthought, "Although I'd rather be under the water than on it."

"What does he think about your new interest in diving?"

"He's been pretty good. He's given me a few lectures on ecological responsibility. And of course I agree with him all the way. But he hasn't said too much—I guess he sees how much I like it."

Melissa mused that Benny's interest had changed him, and for the better. There was a new, if embryonic, confidence in his attitude. Even his speech reflected it. He no longer seemed to feel the need to impress listeners with his knowledge of four-syllable words; he talked quite plainly, as if his only desire were to communicate in the simplest, most direct way possible. He surely could not have changed so much in the two weeks she had been gone; perhaps she had simply been too preoccupied to notice the gradual transformation. At any rate, she was gratified and happy for him.

Highcliffe Inn was in its hour of late-afternoon somno

lence. Doris Emerson was behind the desk and waved cheerfully. They hurried up the stairs, Benny delivering the luggage to Melissa's room while she went into the family sitting room.

Paul Starbuck was stretched out on the sofa dozing under his newspaper. The pages scattered as he opened his eyes and got up precipitately when he became aware of his daughter's presence.

"Honey, it's good to have you back." His voice was deep with emotion.

She ran to him and hugged him tightly. "Oh, Dad, it's good to be back."

In those two simple sentences, spoken slowly and haltingly, much was understood between them. An unspoken truce was declared. They would try to be as close as ever, but certain subjects would be off limits for the present, the first and foremost being Rod Wilshire. It was safer and simpler that way.

Melissa felt weak with relief that she and her father had made a kind of tacit peace. The status of her relationship with Rod was so confused at the moment, even in her own mind, that it was better if nothing was discussed directly. It might not be so easy to avoid discussion with her mother, but for that she would have to wait and see.

She looked briefly around the room. "Where's Mother?"

"Over past Star Point, collecting wild flowers. She's become a fanatic about gathering and drying those things. Now she's talking about starting a business selling them this fall when she goes back to New York."

"Why not?" Melissa thought her mother could probably make a go of it. Ellen had a shrewd head for business in addition to her considerable artistic gifts. "When are we going sailing, Dad?"

"Oh, not later than Sunday morning, weather permitting."

"Why? Is it supposed to turn bad?"

156

"There've been rumors on the radio this morning about a storm blowing up the coast. Probably turn out to be a false alarm—they usually are."

Ellen Starbuck returned, her arms laden with two large baskets overflowing with trumpet-shaped day lilies. "Welcome back, darling!" she cried to Melissa, setting the flowers aside. "We missed you. You're here for the rest of the summer now, I hope."

"Yes, indeed, what's left of it. Mr. Hartstone assured me there would be no more dream sequences. My character will be exonerated and freed from prison in late September, and I'll rejoin the show as a fully vindicated, upstanding member of the community."

Ellen smiled at her daughter lovingly. "I'm glad they believe in happy endings," she said softly, hugging Melissa closely. "Everybody deserves one . . . no one more than you."

Melissa glanced at her mother quickly. There was a quiet knowingness in the older woman's voice. Had Ellen managed to guess from their last telephone conversation that something was amiss between Melissa and Rod? But Ellen said no more, and Melissa decided it was only her imagination.

She went downstairs to the kitchen, where she got a big embrace from Sally Emerson.

"I think you lost a little weight down there off-island. We'll have to fatten you up." Sally held her at arms' length and raked her eyes pitilessly over Melissa's body. "You're not as big as a peanut. I bet you've lost ten pounds."

"Hard work, Sally." Melissa laughed. *And sleepless nights,* she thought. "What can I help you do?"

"Not one thing. Ellen got another lady to do the vegetable chopping and washing-up, so we're in fine shape. You better go rest yourself before dinnertime. You look like you could use it."

Melissa wandered out to the porch. The dining deck had been completed, and she silently applauded the result:

brilliant floral tablecloths; on each table small vases filled with a sprig of Ellen's wild flowers. Between the broad windows hurricane lamps glowed a pinkish amber. And outside, as a backdrop for the diners' eyes and ears, the surf of Nantucket Sound rolled in. It was, she thought, enchanting.

She looked out over the sound, shielding her eyes against the interior light, and wondered where Rod was at that moment. Then she told herself she had no right to wonder. The final rupture between them had been her choice, not his. She would have to send the ring back to him again, and this time the break would be permanent.

She and her father went sailing on Sunday morning. Melissa had hoped her brother would join them—she was really enjoying the new Benny. But he declined regretfully, saying that Sunday was the busiest day of the week at The Sunken Vessel, and his presence was essential.

When she saw the *Ellenissa* at the end of the Highcliffe jetty, she shrieked with pleasure. The sailboat had been given a glossy new coat of varnish, and when they began unfurling the mainsail, she saw that it was new as well.

"Such extravagance," she reproached her father with mock sternness.

"Well, I don't know if you've noticed, but Highcliffe Inn is now booked solid, and apparently will be for the rest of the season. So we're doing all right, honey."

Melissa kissed her father on the tip of his nose. "That's great, Dad. But I hope you're letting somebody else do most of the work."

"You better believe it. You've all spoiled me rotten, and now that I've got in the habit of doing nothing, I've learned to love it."

"Good! I couldn't have better news."

Paul adjusted the jib, and they headed north into the sound. Melissa tried to make the suggestion casual: "Let's

158

sail out and take a look at that equipment from Oceanic, Dad. You know, the—"

"Oh, that's a good distance farther out, honey. We better not go out that far today. Weather's too unpredictable."

"Did you find out any more about what they were doing out there?"

"No. I decided I couldn't police the entire Atlantic, giving out summonses every time someone threw a beer can overboard, so I'd better relax and try to forget about it."

Melissa was relieved that his attitude had softened. Perhaps she could, by treading gingerly, hint at the information about Rod that Jim Wilson had given her. "I happened to run into Jim Wilson at the Woods Hole side of the ferry yesterday," she began.

"Yes?" Her father's voice was wary but noncommittal.

"He told me Rod wasn't involved in this project, Dad. I think Jim and Jerry and a couple of the other former members of Rod's crew are doing it on their own. Rod's working on something entirely different."

Paul Starbuck looked at her in disbelief. "From what I've seen of that crew, Rod would have to be involved in it—he's the only one with brains enough to direct an operation like that. Jim Wilson and his brother are hardly out of diapers."

She could not help smiling at her father's hyperbole, although she was somewhat distressed at his insistence that Rod was indeed involved. "I wouldn't say that. Jim and Jerry Wilson are only two or three years younger than I am. You wouldn't accuse me of being barely out of diapers, would you?"

"You're advanced for your age." His eyes crinkled in a grin. "And sometimes I wonder about you." He broadened the grin to let her know he was teasing her.

"Oh, Dad, you're impossible."

And he was. She had somehow let him get her off the

159

track of what she intended to be a serious conversation. While she tried to think of a way to bring the subject back to Rod's innocence, she realized that the wind propelling the boat was blowing rather fiercely. There was little time for further talk, for Paul was kept busy tacking first to starboard and then to port, operating the mainsail and yelling instructions to Melissa on how to swing the jib. Melissa worried that he was overexerting himself, but he seemed to be taking great pleasure in the skillfulness of his maneuvers.

"Are we going on to Madaket?" she called. Full voice was needed to be heard above the wind.

"No, I think we'd better call it a day. I guess they mean business about the storm this time."

But by the time they got back to port, the wind had diminished and the sea was almost placid. Apparently the storm was going to bypass the island after all.

That evening they heard on the news that the storm would miss the island and had moved out into the Atlantic. Nantucket innkeepers and shop owners breathed a collective sigh of relief and abandoned their plans to board up windows and sandbag walls.

Melissa awoke in the dead of night. Something was bothering her, and she had no idea what it was. Then she realized the ring, which she was still wearing, was digging into her cheek. She had apparently been sleeping with her hand cushioning her face, and the projection of the stone had become uncomfortable enough to awaken her. *That must be an omen of some kind,* she thought unhappily. *I'll take it back to him tomorrow.* Her family had so far not questioned her about Rod; perhaps they would continue to keep their counsel, even when they realized she was no longer wearing his ring.

She slept another restless two or three hours and finally concluded she might as well get dressed and go downstairs. Benny was on the dining deck, having a bowl of cereal before going off to his job. Melissa joined him, setting her cup of coffee down with a somewhat unsteady hand.

"What's the matter with you, Liss?" Benny asked in mild surprise.

"Nothing. I'm fine. Had a little trouble sleeping is all."

Benny glanced at the ring as its facets caught the pale early-morning sun. Then he jerked his head up sharply in sudden realization. "You haven't seen Rod Wilshire since you've been back, have you? Isn't that a little strange?"

Melissa blinked rapidly. She could not burst into tears in front of her brother, yet that was precisely what she had an impulse to do. Nor could she tell him yet that he had been right about Rod's womanizing.

"He's—he's very busy right now. I'll be getting in touch with him soon."

"Yeah, I guess he is busy. I don't know what he's doing, but it must be something superimportant."

Melissa was instantly alert. "Why do you say that?"

"Last week we had to deliver some equipment to the Coast Guard station out by 'Sconset. Then we had another delivery to make up in Quidnet. Just after we passed the Sankaty Head Lighthouse, a bunch of coastguardsmen stopped us and said we'd have to take a detour. When we asked them why, they said it was orders. Anyway, we had to go way inland and then get back on Quidnet Road. This guy in Quidnet we delivered the stuff to—the place was swarming with divers—said they were on a government project and nobody was allowed anywhere near it."

"Oh, really?"

"Yeah. You know, Rod must really be an expert. I'd love to talk to him about diving."

"I thought you didn't care for him, Benny?"

Benny looked slightly abashed. "Oh, I guess I was wrong. He must be a pretty good guy. All that business about Trish must have been my own insecurity."

"Maybe." Melissa wanted to change the subject. "Do

you mind biking into town, Benny? I'd like to use the car for an hour or so. Then I can drop it off at your shop and bike back if you like."

"I've got my own bike now, Lissa, and nearly always use it to go to work. I had the car the other day only because I was picking up some new awnings."

"All right. Then I'll see you later."

She took the car keys from their hook behind the desk and shakily wrote a hurried note:

> Dear Rod,
>   I'm sorry.
>
>   M.

It sounded awkward and abrupt, but she could find nothing else to say.

She drove through the main street of 'Sconset where the roses were, if anything, more lush than those in Nantucket Town. But today their flamboyant beauty went unnoticed. She was looking for Cranberry House, the inn where Rod was staying. She saw it straight ahead on her right and slowed.

It was not yet nine, and the middle-aged woman behind the desk adjusted her spectacles and stifled a yawn as Melissa approached. "Yes, miss, can I help you?"

"You have a Rod Wilshire registered here, don't you?"

"We do indeedy."

"I'd like to leave something for him. But I want to be sure it's put into a safe. It's—it's quite valuable."

"Yes, of course. Come back to the office and you can watch me for yourself."

She watched the velvet box go into the squat black safe and handed the lady the sealed envelope. "You'll be sure he gets this? Just tell him there's something in the safe I left for him."

"Yes indeedy. I'll see to it."

At the entrance that led back into the street, Melissa turned and lingered for one last moment. Was she hoping that Rod would miraculously appear? She only knew she was unwilling to sever the last link with him by walking out the door. As she stood indecisively, the woman seemed to read her thoughts.

"Mr. Wilshire has already left the inn this morning," she said. "He works awfully hard. A nice fellow he is, too."

"Yes," Melissa muttered. "Yes, he's very nice. Well, thank you very much."

"Have a good day, now."

With that futile benediction ringing in her ears Melissa groped her way blindly into the driver's seat of the Volkswagen and remained parked at the curb for several minutes until she could control the shaking of her hands.

Chapter 17

Melissa drove slowly back to Highcliffe Inn, trying desperately to concentrate on the simple act of steering the car. When she walked into the Big Room, she was surprised to find her mother—rather than Doris Emerson—behind the registration desk.

"Doris has an off-island friend visiting, and I don't mind filling in—I kind of enjoy chatting with the guests," her mother explained.

Melissa started upstairs, but Ellen called after her. "Missy, have you got a minute? Come back and talk to me. I want to catch up on your two weeks in New York."

Melissa, noting the childhood appellation, retraced her steps, but with some reluctance. She wanted to have a chance to frame her thoughts into a more coherent whole before she shared them with anyone else.

Her mother began the conversation with casual questions about the television show and how Melissa had survived the Manhattan heat wave. Then she segued smoothly into another subject. "You know, Missy, I had dinner with Rod Wilshire on Monday, after he got back from New York."

"You had dinner with him?" Melissa repeated stupidly. "How did that come about?"

"He simply called and invited me. We went to the Jared Coffin House—it's quite lovely."

The Jared Coffin House. Melissa remembered that that was one of the places where Rod had tried to get a reservation the evening he had presented her with the ring. At the thought of the solitaire she automatically felt for it with the thumb of her left hand, as she had gotten into the habit of doing to assure herself of its presence. Now she was bereft, sensing its absence.

Ellen's eyes followed the gesture, and her face softened with pity. "Melissa, what's this all about? Rod was quite upset and didn't know what to do about it."

"So he had to enlist my own mother as his emissary? Doesn't he have the guts to plead his own case?" Melissa's voice was ragged with sarcasm and fatigue.

Her mother gave a faint smile and an almost imperceptible shake of her head. "I believe he tried to do that in New York, didn't he? With no luck at all, if I'm to believe his story."

"Did he tell you the whole story? About my being—being *accosted* by that girl friend of his? And she had the nerve to ask him when he was going to collect his bathrobe from her apartment!" Melissa's voice wavered. "Mother, it was humiliating. I could have taken it once, but time after time I find he's been involved with—"

"Missy, Rod didn't have a chance to tell you the whole story because you barricaded yourself in your apartment. Now listen"—her mother's voice grew quietly intense—"he felt he owed something to Tracy Nightingale, and it wasn't just because they had been . . . lovers. No, don't interrupt me, Melissa. After Rod's parents died, his godparents took him in and reared him. Those godparents were Tracy Nightingale's aunt and uncle. That's how he met Tracy in the first place.

"Rod had his own money from a trust fund, but they gave him love and security. They were apparently two very remarkable people. Did Rod ever tell you he had polio as a child?"

Melissa shook her head miserably.

"They nursed him back to health from the edge of death," Ellen continued. "When he told you he had a

166

business appointment and then went to help Tracy, he believed he was helping to pay off a very great debt to two people who had given him life itself."

Tears were streaming unchecked down Melissa's face. "I didn't know," she whispered.

Ellen continued in an almost businesslike tone. "He's never pretended you were his first love, has he?"

Melissa shook her head dumbly.

"Then don't try to erase the existence of other women he may have been . . . attached to. It's impossible and you should accept it. I understand the scene with Tracy must have been unpleasant. But don't let pride spoil your whole future. Tracy never implied that she thought Rod was still in love with her, did she?"

Again Melissa shook her head.

"Then why can't you accept his statement that it's over between them? Unless I'm the world's worst judge of character, he's very, very much in love with you, Melissa."

Melissa began to sob. "But I just gave him his ring back. For the second time! It's too late to do anything about it—he'd think I was a complete idiot!"

Ellen opened the Dutch door that separated the desk from the rest of the room; and put her arms about her daughter. "You mean you handed it to him personally?"

"No, I left it in the safe at the place he's staying. He'd already gone out to work." She tried to marshal her thoughts into some semblance of order. "But, Mother, why didn't you tell me this when I first came back?"

"He asked me not to. I suppose he thought it would sound like a bid for pity for the poor little orphan boy. I hope he'll forgive me for betraying his confidence now. But when I see two lovely young people made so wretched by a misunderstanding . . . well, I just couldn't keep quiet any longer."

Trembling, Melissa looked at her mother. "You really think with all your heart he loves me?"

"I know he does."

"Dad still doesn't approve of him."

"Your father can be even more stubborn than his daughter," Ellen said with some exasperation. She took the car keys off their hook where Melissa had replaced them, and gently thrust them into her daughter's hand. "Now go on back to 'Sconset and get your ring. And be on that phone to Rod tonight the minute he gets home from work."

When Melissa stepped from the inn into the outside air, the weather contrasted sharply with the sudden bubbling joyfulness of her mood. A heavy dampness lay over the moors; the sun had vanished behind thickening clouds. It was not until she was halfway to 'Sconset that she became aware of the rising wind; she had trouble keeping the little car on course. But the elements were secondary. Knowing that Rod loved her made her feel invincible enough to control even the wind and the waves.

By the time she got to Cranberry House a light rain had begun to drop from the leaden skies. She was wearing only jeans and a light shirt, and the air was almost chilly. She stepped into the lobby, brushing the misty droplets from her hair. She saw with relief that the same woman was on duty. There wouldn't be any problem with proof of identity or that sort of red tape.

"Hello again," she said chirpily, although her heart was in her throat and she found it almost impossible to swallow. Perhaps Rod had come back early and had already been given the ring. Well, there was only one way to find out. "I—it seems I made a mistake. I'd like to take back the little package I left here earlier."

The lady patted her neatly coifed hair uncertainly. "You want it back, did you say?"

"Yes, please."

The woman examined her with a critical eye, then nodded. "I suppose it's all right. You're the one who left it in the first place." She took a large ring of keys from a drawer, then disappeared into the rear office and re-emerged with the blue velvet box. Melissa's breath hissed past her teeth in a sigh of relief.

"You live in 'Sconset?" the woman inquired.

"No, I'm from the Cliff Road area, past Nantucket Town."

"You'd better hurry home, then. That storm they said was headed out into the Atlantic has veered around again."

"Oh, I hadn't heard. Well—thank you very much."

Lucky she had made the trip when she did. With a storm blowing up, Rod would probably be returning to the inn very shortly.

Melissa later had only the faintest memory of the drive back to Highcliffe; it was all a nightmarish blur. Strangely enough, the rain never developed to more than isolated angry spatters. But the wind blew with constant fury. The streets of Nantucket Town were almost deserted, except for merchants boarding up their windows and a few hardy souls who had been caught off guard somewhere and who were now inching their way home, unsteady against the raging wind. It was still early afternoon, but the sky had darkened to an ominous steel-gray. Melissa found it necessary to turn on her headlights.

It was less than ten miles from the village of 'Sconset to Highcliffe Inn, but the journey seemed never-ending. She wondered if Paul and Ellen had bought the hardware needed to repair the storm shutters. Highcliffe, as its name implied, was in a particularly vulnerable location, perched as it was above the sloping palisade.

She drove up the narrow lane and saw that the shutters had been locked in place. That, at least, would offer some protection. She did not leave the car in front but drove it to the rear of the inn where she hoped it would be safe from the gale blowing in angrily from the sound. When she tried to get out of the car, the wind blew her back against the door, and it was only by clinging to the sides of the building that she was able finally to reach the back door and the haven of the warm kitchen.

Sally Emerson called into the Big Room, "She's back!"

Paul and Ellen came into the kitchen, their faces pale with worry. They watched as outside the window a blast of wind lifted the iron weathervane from its foundation and sent it skittering for several feet before it toppled slowly to the ground.

"Where's Benny?" Melissa asked through numb lips.

"He called from the store. He's fine—he'll ride out the storm there." Ellen lowered her voice. "Did you see Rod?"

"No. But I'm sure he's back at the inn by now." Melissa would not permit any alternative thought to enter her mind. "He wouldn't be out in this. I'll call him as soon as it's over."

Though its intensity was fierce, the storm did not last long. By mid-afternoon the darker clouds had scudded away to the western horizon and an anemic white sun was trying to break through the fluffy patches that remained in the mackerel sky. Aside from the casualty of the weathervane and the uprooting of two recently planted trees on the outer reaches of the lawn, Highcliffe Inn survived intact.

When it seemed the calm was a permanent one, Melissa attempted to put through a call to Rod's inn. But she was told by the operator that the lines in 'Sconset were down. She tried to call at half-hour intervals throughout the afternoon and evening, but without success.

"I'm sure you can get through tomorrow, dear," Ellen told her shortly after midnight. Paul had already gone up to bed.

"Yes, I guess so," Melissa replied, and picked up her sweater from the sofa. She was halfway up the stairs when the telephone shrilled loudly.

Ellen, fearful of awaking the guests, hurried to answer.

170

Melissa paused, her hand on the banister. A phone call at this hour could only mean bad news of some kind. When Ellen hung up, she looked up at Melissa, her hands folded vertically in front of her, almost as though she were praying.

"That was a nurse at the Nantucket hospital, Melissa. There's been an accident. Rod has been taken there."

Melissa looked at Ellen with blank disbelief, and her mother added hastily, "The nurse assured me he'll be all right, darling. But she said he wanted her to call you."

Melissa felt a hand on her shoulder and turned to see her father, who had suddenly materialized from the upstairs apartment. He ran the back of his fingers down her cheek lightly.

"I'll take you to the hospital, honey." His quiet voice was matter-of-fact and calm.

Chapter 18

Melissa and her father got into the Volkswagen, and Paul turned on the ignition, finding to his relief that miraculously the car had not flooded. But halfway along Cliff Road an outbuilding had collapsed and blown across the street's entire width, making it impassable.

"Drat," Paul said, shifting the gear into reverse, "I'll try North Beach Street."

Their luck along the alternate route was no better; high water at the street's lowest level was at least two feet deep.

"We'll have to go back, Lissa. There's just no way."

Melissa nodded resignedly, absently. She had already seen that the road was washed out, and was remembering the last time she had been driven in desperate haste to the Nantucket hospital. The situations of the two men involved had been reversed, for on that earlier night Rod had driven her in to see her father.

They drove back, then mounted the stairs in weary defeat.

At the door to her bedroom Paul said, "Wait, Lissa. I'm going to bring you a sleeping pill. No, no protests. Your staying awake all night won't do Rod any good, and it'll do you a lot of harm. We'll try again tomorrow."

Comforted to some extent by that promise, Melissa obediently swallowed the capsule. She got out of her clothes and climbed into bed nude, her arms too heavy to put on a nightgown. Just before she fell asleep she mumbled a half-incoherent prayer, asking forgiveness for her stubborn, foolish pride.

The next morning Ellen reported that Paul Starbuck had had a restless night and she wanted to let him sleep, so Benny drove his sister to the hospital. When Melissa stopped at the nurses' station to check Rod's room number, Benny said, "I'll stay in the lounge, Liss, while you go in. But I would like to see him for a minute before we leave."

Melissa nodded. Her heart seemed to be a huge sledge-hammer assaulting her ribs mercilessly. She did not know whether Rod would even be conscious . . . she had no idea what had happened or how badly he was hurt. When she entered the room, she involuntarily gasped. Rod lay under a sheet, his head swathed in bandages from crown to eyebrows, his eyes closed.

But as she tiptoed across the room, he opened one swollen eye and managed a ghost of a grin. "Don't be alarmed." He spoke slowly through cracked lips. "I'm not the mummy I seem to be. It's only a slight concussion."

"Thank God," she whispered, and knelt by the bed at his side, her face as close to his as the bandages would allow.

She wanted to ask how the accident had happened, but she did not know whether he felt capable of answering questions at the moment. She simply looked at him for a long moment and hoped that her deep, true feeling for him was shining in her eyes.

"I love you, Rod. I've been so foolish. I know that now."

"I'll say you have," he retorted weakly.

A feeling of sweet relief swept through her body. If he felt up to joking, his injuries must not be too serious. The feeling was immediately followed by one of impatience at his foolhardiness.

"Why did you stay out in that storm? I even thought

174

you might have returned before I—" She stopped abruptly.

"Before you what?"

"Well, I mean, I happened to, er, be at Cranberry House just before the storm broke. . . ."

"Cranberry House?" he repeated blankly. "Why?"

She paused and hoped God would forgive the little white lie. "I wanted to ask you if you could forget what a fool I've been for about the last hundred years."

"I'll work on it." He tried to grin.

"Rod, what happened exactly? I mean, if you feel like talking about it—"

He framed his words carefully: "When the storm hit, I was down under about a hundred fifty feet. The weather blew up so quickly, I didn't realize how rough it was on the surface. . . ."

"But how about the others? In the boat? Couldn't they have warned you?"

"They did. They signaled me to come up. But I thought they were only warning me that I had just a few minutes' air left. I knew that. But I thought I needed only a few more seconds—I was trying to scrunch through the—then the wind, I found out later, began to blow the control boat off course—" He sighed tiredly. "Well, it's over for now. I'll try again as soon as I get out of here."

"Oh, dearest, I'm so glad."

He tried to cock an eyebrow, but the bandage foiled his attempt. "What, glad I'll try again?"

"Glad it's over, you idiot, and you're not any more seriously hurt." Her voice broke somewhere between laughter and tears.

He was suddenly somber. "Would you be glad if it—if the diving were over permanently, Melissa?"

She sank into a moment of thought. She remembered the day of the lobster picnic, when Rod had spoken with such deep feeling of the endless fascination of the ocean depths. She could not deprive him of that—it was not only his livelihood, it was his life.

"No." She measured her words. "I think if you gave that up you'd be very unhappy. I wouldn't want to see you trying to live like that."

He adjusted his position on the bed cautiously. "I knew you'd feel that way. That's my Melissa. That's why I love you. Your heart, your spirit, your courage." He thought over the words for a moment, then added slyly, "Not to mention your body."

She laughed and touched the dark stubble on his chin, very lightly, then put her arm over his chest. He winced slightly and gently moved the position of her hand.

"What's the matter?" she asked in alarm.

"Uh, three of my ribs were fractured."

She jerked her arm away guiltily. "Why didn't you tell me?"

"I was so glad to see you it completely slipped my mind." The lopsided grin was as wicked as ever.

"It's good to see you haven't lost your sense of humor," she said dryly. "You'll probably need it before you get out of here."

"Oh, no. I took lessons from your father in how to intimidate hospital personnel. I figure I can wear them down before the week is out."

"Good luck. I think my father only strengthened their resistance." Her face grew serious. "Darling, I have to go. The nurse asked me not to stay long." She remembered Benny's request. "Oh, Benny wanted to say hello. Do you feel up to seeing him for a minute?"

"Of course."

Benny came in tentatively, Rod motioned him close to the bed.

"How you making it, fella? Still at The Sunken Vessel?"

"You bet. Not only that, but when the summer's over I'm going to start contacting oceanographic institutes for next year. When you feel better, I want to ask you about them."

"Sure thing." He gave Benny a speculative glance. "What's your record for staying under? I mean up to this point?"

"Twenty-two thirty."

"You didn't feel any diver's panic or anything like that?"

"Panic?" Benny was puzzled. "I love it down there. What I love most of all are breath-hold dives. I've been doing yoga for a long time, and meditation helps slow the heart, you understand, and—"

Rod nodded in agreement. "Of course. And what's your record for free diving?"

"Two twelve."

"Over two minutes? That's damn good. To what depth?"

Melissa stepped in firmly. "Now look, you two, I can see you're enjoying this shoptalk, but we have to go. We can both come back later."

Benny nodded reluctantly. His eyes were shining from his conversation with Rod. Rod took him seriously and was impressed with his achievements, because Rod knew what they represented. The boy's sneaker-clad feet seemed to float on air as he left the room.

"When will you come back?" Rod asked Melissa wistfully.

"This afternoon. Or tomorrow. As soon as they'll let me."

"Bring Benny with you," he murmured drowsily, and the faintest of smiles played on his lips as he fell into a lightly sedated sleep.

Melissa had just finished lunch the next day when Doris called her to the telephone. Melissa picked up the wall phone by the fireplace in the Big Room.

"Melissa? When are you and your brother getting your-selves down here?"

"Rod? Where in heaven's name are you calling from?" She was certain there had been no phone in his room on the previous day.

"I got a phone in my room this morning. When are you planning to visit?"

"Right away. I'd have come back yesterday, but they told me you'd probably sleep right through till noon to-day. Did you?"

"I did not," he protested indignantly. "I've been busy as a tiny bee since nine this morning."

"Busy? Busy doing what?"

"I'll tell you when I see you. Do you suppose your parents could come along with you?"

"What is this, a conference?" She became serious. "I don't know, Rod. I'll ask them."

"Please do. Tell them I'd like to talk to them both about something."

"What's this grand mystery all about?"

"I'll tell you—all of you—when I see you. Which I hope will be shortly. Visiting hours begin at two, and that's in twenty minutes."

"Yes. Okay. G'bye, darling." Impulsively she blew him a kiss into the phone, feeling faintly silly for having done so. But why not? Why not be gloriously mad and silly and revel in the feeling? Didn't she have every right to be insane with happiness? Rod was going to be all right, and he loved her.

Paul Starbuck grumblingly consented to join her, though Melissa shrewdly guessed that he was flattered to be given a special invitation. Ellen asked them to give Rod her love and promised to visit him the next day, but thought she'd better stay at Highcliffe to mind the store while the others were away.

Melissa was astonished by the improvement in Rod's

178

appearance. Yesterday he had been an invalid—albeit a reluctant one—but today he was propped up jauntily on a thick stack of pillows and flung a cheery salute at the trio as they entered.

Paul went to the bed and offered, with some embarrassment, his wishes for a speedy recovery. Rod thanked him and asked Paul and Benny to find comfortable chairs, patting the bed by his side to indicate Melissa should sit there. Then he began with mock pomposity: "I suppose you wonder why I've called you all together. . . ."

"As a matter of fact, we had," Melissa answered with the same jocundity.

"Seriously, there is something I want to discuss with all of you." He looked first to Paul, his gaze even, straightforward. "Paul, I'm sorry there's been a misunderstanding about what I was doing up here. I know you thought I was on some sort of reckless, irresponsible treasure hunt and was going to ruin the beaches while I was at it."

Paul looked somewhat abashed but also determined to defend his position. "Well, you have to admit Dionis Beach is pretty close to—"

"Wait a minute." Rod turned his head toward Paul carefully. "Dionis Beach? We're nowhere near Dionis—"

"Rod," Melissa jumped in quickly, "Dad thought he saw some Oceanic equipment just off Dionis. He—"

Rod nodded brusquely. "So that's where they were. Well, forget that. Jim and Jerry Wilson quit their jobs, but not before they had reported some of Oceanic's equipment as defective and appropriated it for themselves. They were trying to locate the *Andrea Doria,* can you believe it? When people have gone in with all the money and equipment—well, don't get me started. In any case, they're not there anymore, they're awaiting a grand-jury hearing. I found that out only this morning."

Paul Starbuck had the grace to look apologetic. "I didn't know, Rod, I—"

"Please, no apologies necessary, Paul. I understand

179

your position completely. In fact, there were times—you made things a little rough, you know—when I almost had to bite my tongue to keep from telling you the truth. Now I have permission to do so."

"You have permission?" Melissa repeated. At last they were going to hear the whole story.

"Yes. That's what I've been busy doing this morning." He saw Paul's blank stare. "Well, maybe it won't be so confusing if I start from the beginning:

"Around the first of May a prototype nuclear submarine was launched from the naval station at Groton and headed for Nova Scotia. It carried an amazing instrument on board, a little black box, no bigger than a loaf of bread, which could do many things that up to this time have been accomplished only by the human brain. Unfortunately, the sub encountered a powerful riptide as she rounded the eastern corner of Nantucket, and—though the crew got out okay—she sank.

"That was about the time I was called back from Greece. They needed a diver trained in archaeology who could bring up the black box as though it were the most fragile of two-thousand-year-old relics. Because if extreme care was not taken, the delicate mechanism would be rendered useless."

Paul Starbuck asked quietly, "Are you at liberty to tell us who this 'they' is?"

"As of this morning I am. The federal government."

"Wow," Benny breathed.

"I don't understand still," Melissa offered. "Why are you free to tell us all this now?"

"Because I need your help. Specifically Benny's."

Benny started. "Me? The government needs my help?"

Rod nodded gravely. "That's right. You see, the day of the storm—we had spent over two months trying to locate the sub; it had drifted west half a mile from where it sank—I almost had my hands on the thing. The storm aborted my efforts. But I don't think I could have got it

180

anyway, because the compartments had been compressed by the sinking, and I was simply too big to get into the space. That's where you come into the picture, Benny."

Melissa understood at last, and so did Benny in a dazed kind of way. Paul still comprehended the situation only vaguely; he did not yet appreciate how practiced a diver his son had become.

Benny said, "You mean you want me to dive for it and bring it up?"

"With your parents' okay. I got permission from the authorities this morning to let your family in on the operation, since you're technically a minor. You'll have to be interviewed, sign some papers and stuff like that, of course."

"Oh, boy," said Benny, his tone flat with lingering disbelief that this was happening to him.

Paul interrupted. "Now not so fast, Rod, I have to think this thing over . . . find out precisely what's involved. . . ."

"I wouldn't allow you to go into it in any other way. As soon as I'm out of here, I'll take Benny out to the site. Meanwhile I'll go over the maps with him and we'll plan exactly how it's going to work."

Paul's indignation subsided. "Fine. All right, Rod. We'll see you later. Come on, Benny, my boy."

Paul and Benny left the room, Paul with his arm close around the boy's shoulders.

Melissa leaned over and kissed Rod good-bye. "I'm very proud of you, Rod. I know the situation with my father must have been difficult. After all, you couldn't tell him the truth—you had no way to defend yourself."

"I've had to live through that kind of thing before, Melissa, when I was doing work I wasn't allowed to talk about. But this *was* a special case. I've never before been head over heels in love with my adversary's daughter."

Chapter 19

The following day a government investigator checked into a hotel in the center of Nantucket Town, and from his hospital bed Rod arranged a meeting between the government man and the two male members of the Starbuck family. A few hours after the conclusion of the exhaustive interview, Rod called Benny to tell him he had passed inspection; Benny was beside himself with excitement.

Rod explained to Melissa that afternoon that Benny would try the reclamation first in a diver's suit, but that he might have to do the final phase of the operation in a breath-hold dive. Rod felt that that was perhaps the only way even the rail-thin Benny could reach the severely confined space that held the black box.

Melissa asked then the question that her mother would ask of her a few hours later: "But is he that experienced? He's only been into this diving business for a few months."

"Experience helps, certainly. But mental attitude is equally important. Benny didn't know it at the time, but he's been training for this for years."

"How?"

"His yoga. At some oceanographic schools—especially those doing research on breath-hold dives—it's a regular part of their curriculum."

He looked at her face, which was clouded with concern, and said gently, "Melissa, I'd never ask him to do this if I didn't have every confidence in him. I wouldn't just pick a boy off the street and say, 'Kid, I want you to help me

183

out and take a dive into the ocean for about a hundred and fifty feet.' "

Melissa laughed in spite of herself, and the talk turned to other topics.

For the next few days Benny and Rod worked together for hours, poring over the diagrams, charts, and maps that marked the exact location of the all-important black box in the submerged vessel. The hospital staff agreed that Rod Wilshire was the most trying patient since Paul Starbuck, for they were hard put to thread their way into the room among the scattered documents.

In the mornings before he visited Rod, Benny was taken to the location itself, where he was briefed by the other members of the crew on the particularity of the tides and underwater terrain in that area.

Rod was released from the hospital on Monday, a week after he had entered, and it was decided the salvaging feat would be attempted on Wednesday at low tide, which would occur at five eighteen in the morning. The day before the final preparations were made, Benny's diving suit was given a last careful inspection, and the Starbuck family retired for the night—or for a part of it: their alarms were set for four A.M.

Benny was asleep almost the minute his head hit the pillow. With Rod's help he had become supremely confident of his ability to succeed. Only the other three Starbucks were troubled with fitful, infrequent snatches of sleep.

They drove together to the Coast Guard station off Low Beach Road, where their credentials were minutely checked. Then Melissa and her parents proceeded to the desolate coastline where they would wait while the salvage boat took out Rod and Benny, remaining at the spot until upon completion of the mission, it would bring them back. Dawn was barely beginning to nudge over the horizon.

Ellen Starbuck hugged her son tightly just before he

184

boarded. "I'm proud of you," she said, her eyes swimming.

Melissa said, "I know you can do it, Benny."

Only Paul was silent. He shook Benny's hand but said nothing.

They sat in the car and heard the engine of the boat roar away into the distance.

"You didn't wish him luck, Dad."

Paul Starbuck harrumphed. "I didn't want to make him nervous. I thought he had as much as he could handle with you two women sniffling."

"Male chauvinist," Melissa accused, and the tension was broken.

Rod had refused to give Melissa an estimated time for their return; he said there were too many variables. But Benny thought if all went well, it should not take more than two hours.

The coral sky was becoming incandescent when Melissa heard the roar of a boat. She paid it little attention; not much more than an hour had elapsed. But Paul Starbuck raised his binoculars and adjusted them, gazing out over the expanse of water.

"It can't be their boat yet, can it, Dad?"

"I can't see. The sun's right behind it."

And indeed the huge neon-red ball burnt a fiery path across the water. Melissa and her mother, without binoculars, could see nothing at all.

In a low, strained voice Paul said, "It is them. I can see that blunt cut of the prow. It is them."

They got out of the car and ran to the water. Surely the mission had succeeded or they wouldn't be back so soon. Melissa felt her father's hand on her shoulder.

"You take these," he said and pushed the binoculars into her hands.

She telegraphed her thanks to him, her green eyes full of love. Then she focused the powerful glasses in the direction of the engine's throb, which was growing deeper and louder with every passing microsecond.

A plume of spray crested into the air and over the lenses of the binoculars. She frantically wiped it away and raised the glasses to her eyes again. Within the time that simple action took, the boat seemed to have grown much larger and closer. Now she could see two figures leaning over the frontmost rail. They both had their arms upraised, two fingers of each hand spread in the victory sign.

She lowered the binoculars to clean away a second wash of foam and said, just before an exultant burst of laughter tore from her throat, "They did it."

The accomplishment of the mission was not made public until a week later, when the black box had been delivered safely to who knew where—perhaps Washington, perhaps Groton, perhaps another secure station somewhere. The press releases went into no detail, calling it only "valuable equipment."

For a few days Benny became a sort of folk hero. After it was all over, Melissa learned that he had persuaded Rod to let him dispense with the diver's suit and try the free dive first. He found the box almost at once, detached it, and surfaced in little more than a minute and a half. Even Rod was amazed at the speed with which the feat had been accomplished. When the details of the stunning exploit became known, Benny's picture ran in the Nantucket papers and there was a long article about him in *The Boston Globe*.

August had passed into September, but hardly anyone noticed. The weather remained hot and perfect for the beach; Labor Day brought record crowds streaming in, hungry for the ocean; Highcliffe Inn, where a vacant room was now a rarity, settled back into its busy daily routine.

Rod's injuries had almost completely healed; the only remaining souvenir of his accident was a narrow bandage running just above his left eye, which Melissa thought lent him a rakish, devil-may-care air.

The day he had his final checkup at the hospital, he appeared at Highcliffe Inn without any bandage at all. This was the day Melissa had been dreading, for she knew when he was pronounced fit, he would have to go back to New York to give a detailed, in-person report and, presumably, to be given another assignment.

"Let's take a walk along the beach," he said with that bluntness so typical of him.

"All right." She did not particularly feel like embellishing her statements either.

The slanting light set the crags of the palisade in sharp relief. The air was clear, yet it seemed almost tinted by the rose-red of the sun dropping toward the mainland. They walked down the beach steps toward the sandy coastline where they had had the clambake. So many memories came rushing back that Melissa's happiness was tempered by a rush of nostalgia and poignant longing. This particular summer would never begin again.

"There's something we haven't talked about in a while," Rod said, helping her down the final steps.

"Yes?" She did not know why; she suddenly seemed to be able to speak only in monosyllables.

"At one time we had plans for a fall wedding."

She looked at him, bit her lip, then searched the sand as if looking for some divine revelation. At last she found her tongue: "I can't leave until later in the month, Rod, and by that time you might be on the other side of the world."

He started laughing, then tipped her face up and forced her to look at him. "Sweetheart, don't you think they ever let me off the leash? I've already told them I'm having a month's vacation after I make my report. I've also told them that when I do take a job, I won't work outside the continental United States for at least a year. Don't you

187

think that gives us time to squeeze in a honeymoon some-where along the line?"

"But when the government orders you to do something . . ."

"I don't work for the government. Oceanic Surveying gets government contracts and does whatever is required. I'm not even primarily a diver—I'm an archaeologist. But as they said, it's easier to train an archaeologist to become a diver than to make a diver into an archaeologist."

"Oh." She breathed a rushing sigh of understanding and relief.

On a vibrant blue October day in New York City Rod and Melissa were married. The wedding was not large—fewer than a hundred guests watched her walk down the aisle in an afternoon dress of oyster-colored silk, her red hair captured by a bandeau of tiny seed pearls.

After a reception at Rod's club the couple spent their first night at the Plaza, before getting a noon plane to Portugal the following day. It was a country—they had discovered in conversation a few weeks before the wedding —that had long entranced them both.

The bellboy left their bags on the luggage rack and accepted with a courteous nod the bill Rod proffered.

Melissa glanced about the beautifully appointed baroque suite with delighted curiosity. "I've never been in a room at the Plaza before."

"You'd better cut out the daydreaming," Rod warned her with feigned severity. "We have reservations at Lutèce for eight thirty."

"Oh, yes, I'd forgotten." She laughed. "Imagine forget-ting a little thing like dinner at Lutèce."

She changed into a sea-green chiffon cocktail dress, deeply scooped and draped at the neck, its skirt floating behind her like a whisper.

Rod got up from the sofa as she entered the sitting room, and emitted a soft whistle. "My God," he said.

"You get more beautiful every time I look at you. Within a week I'll be just a small puddle of adoration at your feet."

"Idiot." She smiled, then saw the champagne chilling in a silver bucket on the coffee table. "I thought we had to hurry."

"I called and made the reservations for nine thirty. You don't mind, do you?"

"I'll try to bear up."

He poured the sparkling wine and handed her goblet across the table.

"Here's to us and all the other happy lovers in the world," he said, grinning.

"And all the people who were once happy lovers, and all the others who will one day be happy lovers." She was struck by a flash of memory. "Remember what I said the night of the clambake?" she asked. "I said, 'I can't believe life can be this perfect, can you?' And you said, 'It isn't very often.' "

"So I did," he agreed soberly. "But I think, Melissa, my darling, we'd better both begin to realize that occasionally —just very occasionally—it is."

He rounded the table and came to her. He took her champagne goblet and set it down. His eyes never left hers as he came back to her and took her in his arms. He kissed her eyelids, her ears. When at last his mouth found her lips, she was afloat in a throbbing universe where time no longer existed. His tongue flicked hers with light, quick thrusts. He pulled her to the sofa and her hair loosened into a soft cloud about her face. She felt the solidness of his chest, its weight on her body a glorious burden. She had thought the night in her apartment enchanted, but she realized now it had been only a prelude to the wonderful subtlety and variety of his caresses.

His mouth found the rich valley between her scented breasts, and he explored the soft flesh with tantalizing delicacy. Melissa felt helpless against the excitement

189

seething inside her, and with her hand she hungrily guided his head to meet her mouth again.

When at last they separated, he breathed, "I'm crushing your beautiful dress."

She gave him a sly sidewise glance. "Then I'd better take it off, hadn't I?"

He lifted an eyebrow ever so slightly. "That might be a very good idea." He moved to the telephone. "And while you're doing that, I'll phone Lutèce and change the reservations."

"To when?"

"Well, if they aren't still serving at two A.M.—and I don't think they will be—there's an all-night hamburger place down the street." He looked at her quizzically. "But from Lutèce to McDonald's is quite a comedown on your wedding night, isn't it?"

As the last button gave way to her eager fingers she turned to face him, all the wide-eyed ingenue. "I *love* hamburgers," she said.

LOOK FOR NEXT MONTH'S
CANDLELIGHT ECSTASY ROMANCES™:

Love—the way you want it!

Candlelight Romances